THE
MILLIONAIRE'S
ROYAL RESCUE

THE MILLIONAIRE'S ROYAL RESCUE

BY

JENNIFER FAYE

MILLS
BOON

First published in Great Britain 2017
By Mills & Boon, an imprint of HarperCollins*Publishers*
1 London Bridge Street, London, SE1 9GF

Large Print edition 2017

© 2017 Jennifer F. Stroka

ISBN: 978-0-263-07117-7

Our policy is to use papers that are natural, renewable and recyclable products and made from wood grown in sustainable forests. The logging and manufacturing processes conform to the legal environmental regulations of the country of origin.

Printed and bound in Great Britain
by CPI Antony Rowe, Chippenham, Wiltshire

For Mona and Louie.
Thanks for the smiles and the reminder
that there's more to life than work.
I hope your dreams come true.

PROLOGUE

ANOTHER DISASTROUS DATE.

Lady Annabelle DiSalvo's back teeth ground together as memories from the night before came rushing over her. It was tough enough finding a decent guy who liked her for herself and not for her position as the daughter of the Duke of Halencia, but then to expect him to put up with her overzealous security team was another thing altogether.

And so when her date had tried to slip away with her for a stroll beneath the stars, her bodyguard had stopped them. Heat rushed to Annabelle's face as she recalled how the evening had ended in a heated confrontation between her, him and her unbending bodyguard. It had been awful. Needless to say, there'd be no second date.

The backs of Annabelle's eyes stung with tears of frustration. She couldn't stand to live like this any longer. Her friends were all starting to get married, but she was single with no hope of that changing as long as her every move was monitored. She just wanted a normal life—like her life had been before her mother's murder.

If only her mother were here, she could talk some sense into Annabelle's overprotective father. She missed her mother so much. And the fact that her father rarely spoke of her mother only made the hole in Annabelle's heart ache more.

She clutched her mother's journal close to her chest. Maybe she shouldn't have been snooping through her mother's things, but her father had left her no other choice. How else would she ever really get to know her mother?

Annabelle slipped the journal into her oversized purse and rushed down the sweeping staircase of her father's vast estate in Halencia. At the bottom of the steps her ever-vigilant bodyguard, Berto, waited for her. There was actually a whole team of them, all taking turns to protect Annabelle.

Ever since her mother had died during a mugging, Annabelle had been watched, night and day. And since her mother's murderer had never been caught, Annabelle had understood her father's concerns at the time. But now, eleven years later, the protective detail assigned to her felt claustrophobic and unnecessary.

She'd thought by moving to Mirraccino, her mother's home country, that things would change, but with the king of Mirraccino being her uncle, she was still under armed guard. But Annabelle had a plan to change all of that. And she was just about to put that plan in motion.

"Berto, I'm ready to go."

The man with short, dark hair and muscles that were obvious even with his suit jacket on, got to his feet. He was the quiet sort and could intimidate people with just a look. Annabelle was the exception.

She'd known him since she was a teenager. He was a gentle giant unless provoked. She thought of him as an overprotective big brother. They moved to the door. Annabelle was anxious to get back to Mirraccino for a pivotal business meeting—

"Not so fast," the rumble of her father's voice put a pause in her steps. The Duke of Halencia strode into the spacious foyer. His black dress shoes sounded as they struck the marble floor. "I didn't know you were leaving so soon." He arched a brow. "Any reason for your quick departure?"

"Something came up." Her unwavering gaze met her father's.

He tugged on the sleeves of his suit, adjusting them. "What's that supposed to mean?"

"It means I have responsibilities in Mirraccino. Not that you would understand." Her voice rose with emotion as memories of last night's date flashed in her mind.

"Annabelle, I don't understand where this hostility is coming from. It's not like you."

"Maybe it's because I'm twenty-four years old and you will not let me live a normal life."

"Of course I do—"

"Then why do you refuse to remove my bodyguards? They're ruining my chances of ever being happy. Momma's been gone a long time. There is no threat. All of that died with her."

"You don't know that." Her father's dark bushy brows drew together and his face aged almost instantly.

Her patience was quickly reaching the breaking point. "You're right, I don't. But that's nothing new. I've been asking you repeatedly over the years to tell me—to tell both myself and Luca why you're worried about us—but you refuse."

Her father sighed. "I've told you, the police said it was a mugging gone wrong."

"Why would a mugger come after us?"

"He wouldn't."

"But?" He couldn't just stop there.

"But something never felt right."

At last some pieces of the puzzle were falling into place. "Because her jewelry and wallet were taken, the police wrote it off as a mugging, but you know something different, don't you?"

Her father's lips pressed together as his dark brows gathered. "I don't know any more than the police."

"But you suspect something. Don't you?" When he didn't respond, she refused to give up. This was too important. "Poppa, you owe me an explanation."

He sighed. "I found it strange that your mother phoned me from the palace to say something was not as it seemed, but she wouldn't go into details on the phone. And two days later, she...she's killed in a mugging."

"What wasn't as it seemed?"

"That's it. I don't know. It might have been nothing. That's what the police said when I told them. All of the evidence said it was a mugging."

"But you never believed it?"

He shook his head. "When the king didn't know what your mother had been referring to, I hired a private investigator. He combed through your mother's items and talked with the palace staff. He didn't come up with anything that would have gotten her killed."

"Maybe the police were right."

Her father shook his head. "I don't believe it."

"Even though you don't have any evidence?"

"It's a feeling." His face seemed to age right before her. "And I'm not taking any chances with you and your brother. You two are all I have left."

"I know you're worried but you can't continue to have us followed around and spied upon like we're criminals. It's so bad Luca never comes home anymore. And—" She thought of admitting that was why she still lived in Mirraccino, but the pain reflected in her father's eyes stopped her.

"And what? You just want to go about as though nothing happened? There's a murderer still on the loose."

Annabelle had placated him most of her life because she felt sorry for him as he continued to grieve for her mother. However, living in Mirraccino for these past couple of years had given her a different perspective. If she didn't stand up for herself, she would never gain her freedom. She would never be able to experience a lot of her dreams. She would forever live under her father's thumb and that was not truly living.

Many people were put off by her security detail. She ended up refraining from doing things just because it was easier than following security protocol and having people send her strange looks, not to mention the whispered comments. Most guys she might have a chance with quietly backed off after meeting Berto. The ones that persisted, she'd learned the hard way, were trouble, one way or the other. And so her dating life was sporadic at best.

"I'm not backing down, Poppa. I'm twenty-four now. I deserve to have my own life—"

"You have a life."

"No, I don't. My every move is analyzed before I do it. And then it is reported back to you. That is not a life."

Her father sighed. "I'm sorry you feel that way, but I'm just doing what I must to protect you and your brother. I don't hear him complaining."

"That's because Luca doesn't care what you or anyone says. He does exactly what he wants."

Her father ran a hand over his clean-shaven jaw. "I know. I know."

"Is that what you want me to do?"

"No!" Her father's raised voice reverberated off the walls.

"Then maybe you need to back off. I'm not wild like Luca, but if that's what you want—"

"Don't you dare. I have enough problems with your brother, but that's going to come to an end. If he wants to inherit my title, he has to earn it."

She couldn't help her brother, not that Luca would want or accept her help, but they were getting sidetracked. "My brother can fight his own battles. This is about you and me. I need you to back off or…"

Her father's gaze narrowed. "Or what?"

She didn't have an answer to that question. Or did she? There was something that had come to mind more than once when she'd felt smothered.

"Or else you'll leave me no choice. I'll leave Halencia and Mirraccino." She saw the surprise reflected in her father's eyes. She hated to do this to him, but perhaps that's what it would take to get her father to understand that she meant business.

He didn't say anything for a moment. And when he did speak, his voice was low and rumbled with agitation. "Your threats won't work."

"Poppa, this isn't a threat. It's a promise. And it's not something that I take lightly."

Her father stared at her as though gauging her sincerity. "Why don't you and your brother understand that I just want to protect you?"

"I know you are worried about our safety after… after what happened to Momma, but that was a long time ago. It was just a mugging—there's no threat to us. You can relax. We'll be safe."

He shook his head. "You don't know that. I can't remove your security detail. I…I have to be sure that you're mature enough—competent enough—to take care of yourself."

The knowledge that her father thought so little of her stabbed at her. But she refused to give in to the pain. This was her chance to forge ahead. "I will prove to you that I'm fully capable of taking care of myself and making good decisions."

Business was something her father understood and respected. She told her father how she'd taken over the South Shore Project. With the crown prince now occupied with his new family and assuming more and more of the king's duties, he didn't have time to personally oversee the project. And Annabelle had happily stepped up. And she almost had the entire piazza occupied. There was just one more pivotal vacancy that needed to be filled. And not just by anyone, but a business that would draw the twentysomething crowd—the people with plenty of disposable cash that would keep the South Shore thriving long into the future.

"And you think you can do this all on your own?" There was a note of doubt in her father's voice.

Her back teeth ground together. Her father was so old-fashioned. If it were up to him, she'd be married off to some successful businessman who could help sustain her father's citrus business.

Annabelle lifted her chin as her gaze met his.

"Yes, I can do this. I'll show you. And once I do, you'll remove the bodyguards."

Their gazes met and neither wanted to turn away. A battle of wills ensued. Obviously her father hadn't realized that he'd raised a daughter who was as stubborn as him.

All the while, she wondered if there was any truth to her father's suspicions about her mother's death. Or was he just grasping for something more meaningful than her mother had died over some measly money and jewelry?

CHAPTER ONE

THIS DAY WAS the beginning of a new chapter...

Lady Annabelle DiSalvo smiled as she walked down the crowded sidewalk of Bellacitta, the capital of Mirraccino. Though the day hadn't started off the way she'd hoped, she had high hopes for the afternoon.

With a few minutes to spare before her big meeting, she planned to swing by Princess Zoe's suite of offices. They had become good friends since Zoe and the crown prince had reconciled their marriage. Annabelle admired the way Zoe insisted on being a modern-day princess and continued with her interior design business—although her hours had to be drastically reduced to accommodate her royal duties as well as being a wife and mother. If Zoe could make it all work, so could Annabelle. She just had to gain her freedom from her father's overzealous security.

It wasn't until then that Annabelle recalled the email Zoe had sent her. Zoe had left town with her husband on an extended diplomatic trip. And with the other prince in America, visiting with his wife's family, the palace was bound to be very quiet.

Someone slammed into her shoulder. Annabelle struggled not to fall over. As she waved her arms about, the strap of her purse was yanked from her shoulder. Once her balance was restored, her hand clenched the strap.

No way was this guy going to get away with her purse—with her mother's final words in a journal lying at the bottom of the bag. For the first time ever, Annabelle regretted forcing Berto to walk at least ten paces behind her. This was all going down too fast for him to help.

Knowing the fate of the journal was at stake, she held on with all of her might. But the short lanky kid with a black ball cap was moving fast. His momentum practically yanked her arm out of its socket.

Pain zinged down her arm. The intense discomfort had her fingers instinctively loosening their grip. And then they were gone—the purse, the journal and the thief.

"Hey! Stop!" Annabelle gripped her sore shoulder.

"Are you okay?" Berto asked.

"No. I'm not. Please get my purse! Quick!"

The man hesitated. She knew his instructions were to stay with her no matter what, but this was different. That thief had her last connection to her mother. Not wasting another moment while the culprit got away, Annabelle took off with Berto close on her heels.

"Lady Annabelle, stop!" Berto called out.

No way! She couldn't. She wasn't about to let another piece of her past be stolen from her. The hole in her heart caused by her mother's death was still there. It had scar tissue built up around it, but on those occasions when a mother's presence was noticeably lacking, the pain could be felt with each beat of her heart.

Annabelle's feet pounded the sidewalk harder and faster. "Stop him! Thief!"

Adrenaline flooded her veins as she threaded her way through the crowd of confused pedestrians. Some had been knocked aside by the thief. Others had stopped to take in the unfolding scene.

It soon became apparent that she wasn't going to catch him. And yet she kept moving, catching glimpses of the kid's black ball cap in the crowd. She wouldn't stop until all hope was gone.

"Stop him! Thief!" she yelled at the top of her lungs.

Frustration and anger powered her onward. Berto remained at her side. She understood that his priority was her, but for once, she wished he would break the rules. He had no idea what she was about to lose.

Annabelle's only hope was that a Good Samaritan would step forward and help. *Please, oh, please, let me catch him.*

"Stop! Thief!"

So this was Mirraccino.

Grayson Landers adjusted his dark sunglasses. He strolled down the sidewalk of Bellacitta, admiring how the historical architecture with its distinctive ornate appearance was butted up against more modern buildings with their smooth and seamless style. And what he liked even more was that no one on this crowded sidewalk seemed to notice him much less recognize him as...what did the tabloids dub him? Oh, yes, the slippery fat cat.

Of course, they weren't entirely off the mark with that name. A frown pulled at his lips. He jerked his thoughts to a halt. He refused to get lost on that dark, miserable path into the past.

He scratched at the scruff on his face. It itched and he longed to shave it off, but he really didn't want to be recognized. He didn't want the questions to begin again. The minor irritation of a short beard and mustache was worth his anonymity. Here in sunny Mirraccino he could just be plain old Grayson Landers.

In fact, in less than a half hour, he had a meeting for a potential business deal—a chance to expand his gaming cafés that were all the rage in the United States. Now, it was time to expand into the Mediterranean region.

And Mirraccino offered some perks that had him inclined to give it a closer look. He couldn't imagine that it'd be hard to attract new employees to the sunny island. This island nation was large enough to offer them a choice between city life or a more rural existence. And there was plenty of room on the South Shore for a sizable facility.

His board would love the revenue growth from the international venture. Adding Mirraccino as the hub would give them diversification. It could be the beginning of great things.

"Stop! Thief!" screamed a female above the murmur of voices.

The next thing Grayson knew a young lanky guy bumped into him as he ran up the walk. Grayson reached out, grabbing him as he passed.

The kid yanked, trying to escape the solid hold Grayson had on his upper arm. Between his grip on him and the fact that Grayson had almost a foot on the guy and at least thirty pounds, the kid wasn't going anywhere.

"Thief! Stop him!" again came the female voice and it was growing closer.

Could this guy be the person in question? Grayson gave the teenager a quick once-over. "I'm guessing that's not yours." Grayson gestured to the purse in the kid's hand.

"Yes, it is."

"It's not exactly your color." The purse was brown with pink trim and a pink strap.

The guy continued to struggle, obviously not smart enough to realize that he wasn't going anywhere until the cops showed up. "Let me go!"

Grayson narrowed his gaze on the guy. "If you don't stand still, you won't like what I do next."

"Dude, you don't understand." The kid glanced over his shoulder. "They're after me."

"Probably because you stole," Grayson snatched the purse while the guy wasn't paying attention, "this."

The kid with a few scrawny hairs on his chin turned to him. "Hey, give that back." He glanced over his shoulder again as a crowd formed around them. "Never mind. You keep it. Just let me go."

"I'll keep it and you."

"I called the cops," someone in the crowd called out.

Inwardly, Grayson cringed. The very last thing he wanted to do now was deal with more cops. A little more than a year ago, he'd answered enough questions to last him a lifetime. He was really tempted to let the kid get away and then Grayson could quietly slip into the thickening crowd.

Before he could make up his mind whether to do the right thing for some stranger or protect himself from yet another interrogation, the whoop-whoop of a police car blasted into the air. Then there was the slamming of a car door.

The suspect in Grayson's hold fought for his freedom with amazing force for someone so slight. The punch that landed in Grayson's gut made him grunt. Anger pumped in his veins. No matter what it cost him personally, this guy needed to learn a lesson.

The crowd parted, allowing the police officer to make his way over to them. Thankfully the officer immediately took custody of the feisty young man and restrained him.

"Move aside." A deep gruff voice shouted. "Let the lady pass."

Grayson glanced up to find the most beautiful

young woman standing at the edge of the crowd. Immediately he could see that there was something special about her. Maybe it was her big brown eyes. Or perhaps it was the way her long flowing dark brown hair framed her face. Whatever it was, she was definitely a looker.

It was only then that Grayson noticed the big burly man at her side. Her boyfriend? Most likely. The stab of disappointment assailed him.

Not that he was interested in starting anything romantic. He'd learned his lesson about affairs of the heart—they made you do things you wouldn't normally do and in the end, you got your heart broken, or in his case ripped from his chest. No, he was better on his own.

He was about to turn away when he realized the young woman looked familiar. And then it came to him. She was Lady Annabelle DiSalvo—the very woman he was here to meet with.

The police officer turned to the crowd. "There's nothing here to see. Everyone, please, move on."

Lady DiSalvo didn't move. Was she that fascinated? Or could she be the victim in this case?

This was not the way he'd planned for their relationship to start—their business relationship that was. And then her gaze moved to him. He waited, wondering if she recognized him. Nothing appeared to register in her eyes. And then she turned to talk to the man at her side.

A camera flash momentarily blinded Grayson. *Seriously? Could this day get any worse?*

Where is it?

It has to be here.

Annabelle craned her neck. Her gaze frantically searched for her purse. *Oh, please, let this be the right person. Let him still have my purse.* And then she realized that during the foot chase he could have ditched it anywhere along the way. Her elation waned.

Her gaze latched on to the tall, dark and sexy man standing in the center of the scene. She'd sensed him staring at her earlier. But with those dark sunglasses, she couldn't make out his eyes. He was tall with an athletic build. Her gaze took in the heavy layer of scruff trailing down his jaw, and she couldn't help wondering what he'd look like without it. The thought intrigued her, but right now she had more pressing matters on her mind.

She was about to glance away when she noticed that he was holding her purse. Her gut said he wasn't the thief. The young man next to him giving the policeman a hard time was wearing a dark ball cap. That had to be the culprit. The kid had the right build as well as a smart mouth.

"Hey you! That's my purse!" Annabelle called out, hoping the stranger would hear her. "I need it back."

A reporter positioned himself between them. The man with her purse began backing away and turning his face away from the camera. What was up with that?

She had to get to the man with her purse. And it'd probably go better if she didn't have Berto in tow. Even though she knew he was a gentle giant, strangers found his mammoth size and quiet ways a bit off-putting.

While Berto glanced over the crowd for a new threat, she quietly slipped away. She threaded her way through the lingering crowd. There was a lot of *pardon me* and *excuse me*. But finally she made her way over to the man with her purse in his hand just as the officer was escorting the thief to the police car.

Annabelle had to crane her neck to gaze into the man's face.

"Thank you so much. I didn't think I'd ever see my purse again. You're quite a hero."

The man looked uncomfortable with her praise. "I'm glad I could help."

"Well, I really appreciate it."

"No big deal."

It was a huge deal, but she didn't want to get into any of that right now. "If you'll just give me my purse, I'll be going."

Even standing this close to the man, she couldn't make out his eyes through the large, dark sunglasses. His brows rose in surprise, but he didn't make any motion to give it back.

"Is there a problem?"

"I can't hand it over." The man's voice was deep and smooth like a fine gourmet coffee.

He couldn't be serious. She pressed her hands to her hips. "I don't think you understand. That's my purse. He," she gestured to the thief, who was struggling with the police officer, "stole it from me."

"And it's evidence. You'll have to take it up with the police."

Really? He was going to be a stickler for the law. "Listen, I don't have time for this. I have a meeting—"

"I have to give this to the police. I'm sorry." There was a finality to his tone.

What was it with this day? First, there was the scene with her father. Then she missed her flight. And if that wasn't enough, she'd nearly lost her mother's journal. And now, this man refused to return her belongings.

Maybe she just needed to take a different approach. "If it's a reward you want, I'll need my purse back in order to do that."

The man frowned. "I don't need your money."

This couldn't be happening. There had to be something she could say to change his mind before the policeman turned his attention their way. At last, she decided to do something that she'd never done before. She was about to play the royalty card. After all, desperate times called for desperate measures. And right now, she was most definitely desperate.

But then she had a thought. "If I don't file charges, it's not evidence."

"You'll have to take it up with the officer."

Seriously. Why was the man so stubborn?

"Do you know who I am?"

Before the man could respond, the policeman strode over to them. "I'll be taking that."

The mystery man readily handed over her purse. She glared at him, but she didn't have time to say anything. Her focus needed to remain on getting the journal back.

"That's my purse. I need it back," Annabelle

pleaded with the officer. "All of my important things are in there."

"Sorry, miss. Afraid it's evidence now." When the young officer glanced at her, the color drained from his face. "Lady Annabelle, I didn't know it was you. I…I'm sorry."

She smiled hoping to put him at ease. "It's all right. You're just doing your duty. As for my purse, could I have it back now?"

Color rose in the officer's face. His gaze lowered to the purse in his hand. "The thing is, ma'am, regulations say I have to turn this in as evidence. My captain is always telling us to follow the regs. But seeing as it's you, I guess I could make an exception—"

"No." The word was out of her mouth before she realized what she was saying—or maybe she did realize it. She didn't want this young man getting in trouble with his captain because she had him break the rules. "You do what you need to do and I'll come by the police station to pick it up later."

The officer's eyes widened in surprise. "Much appreciated, ma'am, especially seeing as you're the victim. I'll need you to file a complaint against the suspect."

"I…I'm not filing charges."

The officer frowned at her. "That would be a mistake."

He went on to list the reasons that letting the kid get away with this crime would be a bad idea. And he had some good points. In the end, she had to agree with him.

"Okay. I'll need you and the man who caught the thief to make statements down at the station." The officer glanced around. "Where did he go?"

She glanced around for her hero, but there was no sign of him. How could he vanish so quickly?

"I didn't get a chance to catch his name much less take a statement." The officer shook his head as he noted something on the pad of paper in his hand.

Why had the man disappeared without giving his statement? Was he afraid of cops? Or was it something else? Something that had him hiding behind dark sunglasses and a shaggy beard?

Or perhaps she'd watched one too many cop shows. She'd probably never know the truth about him. But that didn't stop her from imagining that he was a bad boy, maybe a wrongly accused fugitive or a spy. Someone as mysterious as him had to have an interesting background. What could it be?

CHAPTER TWO

AT LAST SHE'D ARRIVED.

Annabelle checked the time on her cell phone. Luckily, she'd had it in her pocket or it would have been confiscated with her purse. She had two minutes to spare before her meeting with an executive of the Fo Shizzle Cafés. Her name was Mary and they'd corresponded for the past few weeks. It seemed Grayson Landers, the CEO and mastermind behind the hip cafés, was only hands-on once a site had been vetted by a trusted member of his team.

Annabelle took a seat at one of the umbrella tables off to the side of the historic piazza in the South Shore. She glanced around, but there weren't any professional young women lurking about.

Annabelle looked down at the screen of her phone. Her social media popped up. There were already numerous posts about the incident with her purse. There were photos of her, but no photos of her hero's face. Too bad.

And then a thought came to her. Perhaps a phone call to the police station would hurry along the return of her possessions. Her finger moved over the screen, beginning the search for the phone number—

"You're seriously not going to let me through?"

The disgruntled male voice drew Annabelle's attention. She glanced up as Berto blocked a man from getting any closer. She swallowed hard. It didn't matter how many times it happened, she was still uncomfortable having security scrutinize everyone that came within twenty meters of her.

Berto stood there like a big mountain of muscle with his bulky arms crossed and his legs slightly spread. Annabelle had no doubt he was ready to spring into action at the slightest provocation. He'd done it before with some overly enthusiastic admirers. Okay, so having him around wasn't all bad, but she did take self-defense classes and knew how to protect herself.

"You'll have to go around. The lady does not want to be disturbed." There was no waver in Berto's voice.

"I'd like to speak to the lady."

"That's not happening."

Annabelle couldn't see Berto's face, but she could imagine his dark frown. He didn't like anyone messing with his orders and that included keeping strangers at a distance.

Annabelle's gaze moved to the stranger. She immediately recognized him. He was the man who'd rescued her purse from that thief. What was he doing here?

He was a tall man, taller than Berto, but not quite as bulky. The man's dark hair was short and wavy, just begging for someone to run their fingers through it. And those broad shoulders were just perfect to lean against during a slow dance.

He was certainly handsome enough to be a model. She could imagine him on the cover of a glossy magazine. He didn't appear threatening. Perhaps he was interested in her. What would it hurt to speak to him?

Annabelle slipped her phone in her pocket. "Berto, is that any way to treat a hero? Let him through."

There was a twitch of a muscle in Berto's jaw, letting her know he wasn't comfortable with her decision. If it were up to him, her father or even the king, she'd never have a social life. It was getting old. And if this man was bold enough to stand up to Berto, she was intrigued.

Without another word, Berto stepped aside.

The man approached her table. He didn't smile

at her. She couldn't blame him. Berto could put people on edge.

"I'm sorry about Berto. He can be overprotective. I'd like to thank you again. You're my hero—"

"Stop saying that. I'm no one's hero."

"But you stopped that thief and without you, I probably wouldn't have gotten my purse back." Or more importantly, the journal.

"I was just in the right place at the right time. That doesn't make me anything special."

"Well, don't argue with me. It's all over social media." She withdrew her phone. She pulled up the feed with all of the posts that included photos of this man holding her purse, but his head was lowered, shielding his face.

She noticed how the muscles of his jaw tensed. He took modesty to a whole new level. What was up with that? She was definitely intrigued by this man.

"I'm guessing you didn't track me down to claim a reward."

The man in a pair of navy dress shorts and a white polo shirt lowered himself into a seat across the table from her. "You don't recognize me, do you?"

Was this man for real? "Of course I do."

He shook his head. "I meant, do you know my name?"

She was definitely missing something here, but what? "I take it you know me."

"Of course. You are Lady Annabelle DiSalvo, daughter of the Duke of Halencia and niece of the king. Also, you are in charge of the South Shore Project."

If he was hoping to impress her, he'd succeeded. Now, she had no choice but to ask. "And your name would be?"

"Grayson Landers."

Wait. What? He was the genius multimillionaire?

Surely she couldn't have heard him correctly. He removed his sunglasses and it all came together. Those striking cerulean blue eyes were unforgettable—even from an online photo. At the time, she'd thought they'd been Photoshopped. They hadn't been. His piercing eyes were just as striking in person—maybe even more so.

Somehow, someway she'd missed a voice mail or an email because the last she knew she was supposed to be meeting Mary. She swallowed hard. She should be happy about this change of events, but her stomach was aflutter with nerves. She resisted the urge to run a hand over her hair, wishing that she'd taken the time to freshen up before this meeting.

"Mr. Landers, it's so nice to meet you." She stretched her hand across the table.

His handshake was firm but brief. She had no idea if that was a bad sign or not.

"I, uh, wasn't expecting you."

"I know. You were expecting Mary, but my plans changed at the last minute, making it possible for me to attend this meeting."

"I see. I...I mean that's great." She sent him a smile, hoping to lighten the mood.

There was just something about this man that made her nervous, which was odd. Considering who her uncle and her father were, she was used to being around powerful men.

But most of the men in her life wore their power like they wore their suits. It was out there for people to see, maybe not flaunting it, but they certainly didn't waste their time trying to hide who and what they were. But this man, he looked like an American tourist, not a man who could buy a small country. And that beard and mustache hadn't been in any of the photos online.

His brows rose. "Is there something wrong with my appearance?"

Drat. She'd let her gaze linger too long. "No. No. Not at all. In fact, you look quite comfortable."

Her words did nothing to smooth the frown lines marring his handsome face. "Do I need to change for today's meeting?"

"Um, not at all." She jumped to her feet. "Shall we go?"

He didn't say anything at first. And then he returned his sunglasses to the bridge of his nose as he got to his feet. There was something disconcerting about not being able to look into his eyes when they spoke.

The sooner she got this presentation under way, the sooner it'd be over. "Would you like a tour of the South Shore?"

"Yes."

Short and to the point. She wondered if he was always so reserved. She started to walk, thinking about where she should begin. Of course, she'd given this tour a number of times before to other potential business owners, but somehow it all felt different where Mr. Landers was concerned. Everything about him felt different.

Annabelle straightened her shoulders as she turned to the small piazza where an historic fountain adorned the center. "I thought we would start the tour here. The South Shore is a historic neighborhood."

"I see that. Which makes me wonder why you think one of my cafés would fit in?"

"This area has had its better days." She'd hoped her presentation would make the answer to his question evident, but she hadn't even started yet. She laced her fingers together and turned to him. "Where buildings had once been left for nature to reduce them to rubble, there is now a growing and thriving community."

"That's nice, but you haven't answered my question."

She moved closer to the ancient fountain where four cherubs in short togas held up a basin while water spouts from the edge of the fountain shot into the basin. At night, spotlights lit up the fountain, capturing the droplets of water and making them twinkle like diamonds. Too bad she couldn't show him. It was a beautiful sight.

"If you will give me a chance, I'm getting to it."

He nodded. "Proceed."

She turned to the fountain. "This is as old as the South Shore. The famous sculptor Michele Vincenzo Valentini created it. It is said that he visited Mirraccino and fell in love with the island. Wanting to put his mark upon the land he loved, he sculpted this fountain as a gift to its people. The sad thing is that not long after the project was completed, he passed on."

"Interesting." Grayson glanced over his shoulder at Berto. "Will he be coming with us?"

"Yes." Without any explanation about Berto's presence, Annabelle moved toward one of her favorite shops lining the piazza, the bakery. She inhaled deeply. The aroma of fresh-baked rolls and cinnamon greeted her, making her mouth water. Perhaps they should go inside for a sampling. Surely something so delicious that melts in your mouth would put a smile on her companion's handsome face.

"This bakery is another place that's been around for years. In fact, this family bakery has been handed down through the generations. And let me tell you, their baked goods can't be surpassed. Would you care to go inside?"

He didn't say anything at first and she was starting to wonder if he'd even heard her. And then he said, "If that's what you'd like."

Not exactly the ringing endorsement that she'd been hoping for, but it was good enough. And the only excuse she needed to latch on to one of those cinnamon rolls. She yanked open the door and stepped inside. The sweet, mouthwatering aromas wrapped around her, making her stomach rumble with approval. It was only then she realized that due to her flight delay not only had she missed an opportunity to freshen up but she'd also missed her lunch.

After Grayson had enjoyed a cannoli and some black coffee and she'd savored chocolate-and-pistachio biscotti with her latte, they continued the tour. They took in the new senior facility that was housed in a fully refurbished and modernized historic mansion. They walked along the water-front and visited many of the shops and businesses where Annabelle was friends with most everyone.

"This place must be very special to you," Grayson said.

At last, he was finally starting to loosen up around her. She knew fresh pastries and caffeine could win over just about everyone. "Sure. I've been working on the project for two years now. It's given me a purpose in life that I hadn't realized before."

"A purpose?"

She nodded. "I like helping people. I know from the outside it might seem like I'm doing the crown's bidding, but it's a lot more than that. I've been able to help people find new homes here in the South Shore. We created that new seniors' residence. Wasn't that seashore mural in the ballroom stunning?"

"Yes. It was quite remarkable. And it's very impressive how you've taken on this project and found a deeper meaning in it than just selling parcels of land. But I meant you personally—you seem to have a strong link to this place. When you talk about it, your face lights up."

"It does?" Was this his way of flirting with her? If so, she liked it.

"Did you spend a lot of time here as a child? The way you describe everything is way more personal than any sales pitch I've ever heard. And trust me, I've heard a lot of them."

"Well, thank you, I think." She smiled at him, still not quite sure how to take him or the things that he said. "But I didn't spend much time here as a kid. I grew up in Halencia. It's a small island not too far from here." But he was right, this place did have a very familiar vibe to it. She'd noticed it before when she was working but had brushed off the sensation. "My mother grew up here. When she talked about her homeland, it always seemed as though she regretted having to leave here. But as for me, until recently, I only came here for the occasional visit."

"Really? Hmm… I must have been mistaken."

"I think it must just be from me working so closely on this project."

"Of course. Mirraccino seems like it would be a great place for a young family. And that fountain, I can imagine kids wanting to make wishes there. And that bakery, it was fantastic…"

Grayson's voice faded into the background as Annabelle latched on to a fuzzy memory of her mother. They'd been here, in this very piazza the day before her mother was murdered. The memory was so vague that she was having a hard time focusing on it. But she did recall her mother had been upset. She definitely hadn't been her usual happy, smiling self.

"Annabelle? Are you okay?"

Grayson's voice jarred her back to reality. Heat rushed up her neck and settled in her cheeks. She was embarrassed that in the middle of this very important meeting she'd zoned out and gotten lost in her memories. "I'm sorry. What did you say?"

"I can see something is bothering you." He led her over to one of the benches surrounding the fountain and they sat down. "I know we barely know each other, but maybe that's a good thing. Sometimes I find it easier to talk to a stranger about my troubles."

What did she say? That she had some vague

flashback? And why did she have it? What did it even mean?

It was best to deflect the question. "What troubles do you have?"

He glanced away. "We...um, aren't talking about me right now. You're the one who looked as though you saw a ghost."

So he did have a skeleton or two in his closet. Was it bad that she took some sort of strange comfort in knowing that he wasn't as perfect as she imagined him to be, not that she'd done any digging into his past. When she'd done her research on Fo Shizzle, she'd been more interested in his company's financial history and their projections for the future—all of which consisted of glowing reports.

"Annabelle?"

"Okay. It's not that big of a deal. I was just remembering being here with my mother."

His brows drew together. "I don't understand. Why would that upset you?"

She'd told him this much; she might as well tell him the rest. After all, it wasn't like the memory was any big deal. "It's just that the memory is from a long time ago and it's vague. I remember that day my mother wasn't acting like herself. She was quiet and short-tempered. Quite unlike her."

"Was your father with you?"

Annabelle shook her head. "I don't know where he was. I'm assuming back home in Halencia with my brother."

"You have a brother?"

She nodded. "He's six years older than me. But what I don't get is why I'd forgotten this."

"It's natural to forget things that don't seem important at the time. Do you think the memory is important now?"

"I have no idea."

"Why not just ask your mother about it?"

"I can't." Though Annabelle wished with all of her heart that she could speak with her mother.

"You don't get along with her?"

In barely more than a whisper, Annabelle said, "She died."

"Oh. Sorry. If you don't mind me asking, how old were you at the time?"

"I was thirteen. So I wasn't really paying my mother a whole lot of attention."

"I remember what it was like to be a kid. Although I spent most of my time holed up in my bedroom, messing around on my computer."

"So that's how you became so successful. You worked toward it your whole life."

He leaned back on the bench and stretched his

legs out in front of him. "I never set out to be a success. I was just having fun. I guess you could say I stumbled into success."

"From what I've read, you learned to do quite a bit as far as computers are concerned."

"Coding is like a puzzle for me. I just have to find the right connections to make the programs do what I want." He glanced at her. "It's similar to the way you have snippets of a memory of your mother. You need to find the missing parts for the snippets to fit together and give you a whole picture."

Annabelle shrugged and glanced away. "I'm sure the memory isn't important."

"Perhaps. Or maybe it is and that's why you've started to remember it."

"It's not worth dwelling on." Who was she kidding? This was probably all she'd think of tonight when she was supposed to be sleeping. Was there some hidden significance to the memory?

Just then she recalled her mother raising her voice. Her mother never shouted. Born a princess, her mother prided herself in always using her manners.

"You remembered something else."

Annabelle's gaze met his. "How do you do that?"

"What?"

"Read my mind."

"Because it's written all over your face. And just now, you went suddenly pale. I take it whatever you recalled wasn't good."

"I'm not sure."

"Maybe it would help if you remembered a little more. Perhaps it's not as bad as you're thinking."

"Or maybe it's worse." She pressed her lips together. She hadn't meant to utter those words, but the little voice in her head was warning her to tread lightly.

"Close your eyes," Grayson said in a gentle tone.

"What?"

"Trust me."

"How can I trust you when I hardly even know you?"

"You have a point. But think of it this way, we're out here in the open and your bodyguard is not more than twenty feet away. If that isn't enough security, there are people passing by and people in the nearby shops. All you have to do is call out and they'll come running."

"Okay. I get the point."

"So do it."

She crossed her arms and then closed her eyes, not sure what good this was going to do.

"Relax. This won't work otherwise."

She opened her eyes. "You sound like you know what you're doing. Are you some kind of therapist or something?"

"No. But I've been through this process before."

"You mean to retrieve fragmented memories?"

"Something like that. Now close your eyes again." When she complied, he said, "Recall that memory of your mother. Do you have it?"

Annabelle nodded. All that she could see was the frown marring her mother's flawless complexion and the worry reflected in her eyes.

"Now, was it sunny out?"

What kind of question was that? Who cared about the weather? "How would I know?"

"Relax. Let the memories come back to you. Do you recall perhaps the smell of the bakery?"

"I've heard it said that smell is one of the strongest senses—"

"Annabelle, you're supposed to be focusing."

And she was dodging the memories, but why? Was there something there that she was afraid to recall?

She took a deep breath and blew it out. She tried to focus on any detail that she could summon. Together they sat there for countless minutes as she rummaged through the cobwebs in her mind. Grayson was surprisingly patient as he prompted her from time to time with a somewhat innocuous question. These questions weren't about her mother but rather about sensory details—she recalled the scent of cinnamon and how her mother had bought her a cinnamon roll. The sun had been shining and it had taken the chill out of the air, which meant that it was morning.

"And I remember, my mother said she had to speak to someone. She told me to wait on a bench like this one and she would be right back."

"She left you alone?" There was surprise in his voice.

"No. She stayed here in the piazza, but she moved out of hearing range. There was a man that she met."

"Someone you know?"

"I'm not sure. I never saw his face. I just know their conversation was short and he left immediately after they spoke."

"What did your mother say to you?"

Annabelle opened her eyes. "I don't know anymore. I don't think she said much of anything, which was unusual for her. She was always good at making casual conversation. I guess that's something you learn when you're born into royalty—the art of talking about absolutely nothing of relevance."

"At least nothing bad happened."

"Thanks for helping me to remember."

"I wonder what it was about that day that the memory stuck in your mind."

"I'm not sure."

The truth was, it happened a day or two before her mother died. Could it mean something? Had the police been wrong? Was her mother's death more than a mugging? Or was she just letting herself get caught up in her father's suspicions?

Annabelle didn't want to get into details of the murder with Grayson. As it was, she'd exposed more of herself to this stranger than she'd ever intended. It would be best to stop things right here.

CHAPTER THREE

GRAYSON HAD RESERVATIONS.

The site for Fo Shizzle was not what he'd been envisioning.

Sure, what he'd seen so far of Mirraccino was beautiful. Maybe not as striking as Annabelle, but it definitely came in a close second. The South Shore was a mix of history and modernization. The view of the blue waters of the Mediterranean was stunning. But it just didn't seem like the right fit for one of his Fo Shizzle Cafés.

"So what did you think?" Annabelle's voice drew him from his thoughts.

"I think you've done a commendable job with this revitalization project. I think it's going to be a huge success." Now how did he word this so as not to hurt her feelings? After all, she'd been a wonderful hostess. And to be honest, he didn't want this to end. This was the most relaxed he'd felt in more than a year…ever since the accident and the ensuing scandal.

"But…?"

"What?" He'd let his mind wonder and hadn't heard what she'd been saying.

"You like the South Shore, however I detect there's a but coming. So out with it. What isn't working for you?"

He paused, struggling to find the right words. "I was under the impression that the site of the café would be in the heart of the city. This area is nothing like the locations of the other cafés. The way the South Shore was described in the proposal was that it was an up-and-coming area. This," he outstretched his arms at the varying shops, "is very reserved. It's an area that would be frequented by a more mature clientele."

"We are in the process of revitalizing the area—the proposal was a projection. I was certain if I could get a representative of Fo Shizzle here that they would see the potential. I'm sure your café will be a huge draw. I've spoken with the tourism department and they can insert photos and captions prominently in their promo."

His brow arched. He had not expected this bit of news. He couldn't deny that free advertising would help, but would it be enough? "The thing is, my cafés are designed for younger people, high school, college and young adults. The cafés do not cater to a more mature audience. They can be a bit loud at times, especially during an online tournament. The decor is a bit dark with prints of our most popular avatars. Do you know much about our games?"

She shook her head. "Since you can only play on a closed circuit within one of your cafés, I've never had the opportunity. But the research looks intriguing. And I think it would be a hit here with the young crowd."

"To be a success, this area would have to be heavily frequented by young people—"

"And that's what we want." She smiled at him as though she had all of the answers. "I have research studies broken out by demographic."

He liked numbers and charts. "Could I take a look at them?"

She nodded. "Most definitely. I had a copy in my purse, but I also have them at the palace along with an investment package with detailed figures and projections. I wanted you to have a feel for the area before we dove into the numbers."

He glanced around the piazza. "I'm just not sure about this setting. Don't get me wrong—it's beautiful, but it's not quite as urban as our other locations."

"In the reviews I've read about Fo Shizzle, they

say young people come from miles away just to hang out and take part in the high-stakes gaming tournaments. You've definitely latched on to a great idea. And I hear the coffee's not so bad either."

"The coffee is actually quite good." He'd made sure of that. Being a coder, he lived on a steady stream of caffeine when he was on a roll. And he was picky about the flavor. He wouldn't have anything less than the best for his cafés—just as he would only have the top-of-the-line games. The newest titles. And the best quality.

Annabelle gave him a speculative look as though figuring out his unshaven appearance and his longer-than-usual hair. It was not his standard appearance—not unless he was on a deadline for a new program rollout. When it came to business, all else came in a distant second, third or lower ranking.

When she didn't vocalize her thoughts about his appearance, he added, "I'm usually a little more cleaned up." Why was he making excuses for his appearance? It wasn't like he was going to ask her out on a date or anything. Still, he heard himself say, "It's just with the media and all, sometimes it's easier to travel incognito."

She nodded but still didn't say anything.

He hated to admit it, but he really did want to

know what she was thinking. Did he really look that bad? His hand moved to his jaw. His fingers stroked his beard. It was quickly filling in. Soon it would start to get bushy. He didn't warm to the thought.

Beards were okay on some guys, but not him. It just wasn't his thing. "Is it really that bad?"

She shrugged. "It's okay."

Definitely not a ringing endorsement for his new look.

"I guess it doesn't matter much if I shave or not now that my picture is all over social media. And it's not like I'm going to be here much longer—"

"What? You mean you're leaving? Already?"

He nodded. "I have to keep scouting for a head-quarters for my Mediterranean expansion."

"But this is it. The South Shore will be perfect."

Was that a glimmer of worry reflected in her eyes? Surely she couldn't be that invested in doing business with him. And if she was, he had to ask himself why. What was driving her to close this deal?

He cleared his throat. "I'm not ready to make a decision of this magnitude. I have plans to visit Rome, Milan and Athens next."

"And when will you be leaving?"

"In the morning—"

"But you can't." She pressed her lips together as though regretting the outburst.

"Why not?"

"Because you still have to file a report with the police. There's the theft and…and you're an eye-witness. They'll probably want you to testify."

She had a point. And as much as he would like to fly off into the sunset, he wouldn't shirk his duty. "You know, the only reason I walked away is because you said you weren't going to press charges so I figured there was no reason for me to stick around."

"I was truly considering it, but the policeman convinced me it wouldn't be in anyone's best interest. So it looks like you'll be hanging around Mirraccino a bit longer. And I would love to show you more of this beautiful land."

How much more was there to see? And did she really think another day of playing tourist was really going to change his mind?

"I don't know." He glanced at his wristwatch. It was getting late. "Maybe I could swing by the police station now and give them my statement."

"It's Friday. And it's late in the afternoon. I'm sure the people you'll need to speak with will be gone for the weekend or at least have one foot out the door."

"Can't I just give my statement to an officer? Surely the whole police force doesn't go home early for the weekend."

Annabelle smiled. "Funny. But I meant you'll probably have to speak with some of the clerical or legal people."

He nodded. "I suppose they might do things a bit differently from what I'm accustomed to in the States."

Annabelle nodded. "Now let's see about getting you situated."

"I have a room at the hotel in the city."

"I was thinking of something different. How about being a guest at the royal palace?"

Had he heard her correctly? She was inviting him to stay in the palace with the king? "Are you serious?"

"Of course I'm serious. The king is my uncle."

"And you live there—at the palace, that is?"

"At the moment, I do. I've been living there while working in Mirraccino for the past couple of years."

There was a lot about Lady Annabelle that intrigued him. And honestly, what would it hurt if he took a few more days before moving on?

Annabelle was the first person to interest him in a long time—just not romantically. It wasn't that he didn't find her exceedingly attractive. He did. But he refused to get sucked into another relationship. He'd been through enough. His heart was still mending.

"Oh, please say that you'll stay. I've already had a suite made up for you. And…and the King is expecting you at dinner tonight."

"The king wants to meet me?"

Her cheeks bloomed with color and her gaze didn't quite meet his as she nodded.

He suspected she was just saying anything to get him to stay. He had to admit no one had ever dangled an invitation to meet a king before him in order to help with a business deal. What made this amazing woman feel as though she had to jump to such lengths to get him to close this deal?

"Tell the truth," he said. "The king, he isn't expecting me at dinner, is he?"

Her gaze finally met his. "No, but I'm sure it won't be a problem. The suite truly is prepared and awaiting your arrival, as well as the financial projections. We can go over them together if you like."

He couldn't help but smile at the eagerness reflected on her face. "You know, I've never stayed in a palace before." When her eyes widened and her glossy lips lifted into a smile, he said, "We'll just need to pick up my luggage at the hotel and then I'd very much enjoy staying with you—erm, staying at the palace."

A visit to a royal palace, what could possibly go wrong?

Security would be heavy and the paparazzi would be nonexistent. It would be a win-win.

But who would keep him from getting lost in Lady Annabelle's brown eyes?

At last, Annabelle got through on the phone to the police department.

And without playing the royal card, she was able to speak with someone in authority. They told her to stop by in the morning and they'd see about getting some of her possessions back to her. She wasn't sure what *some* consisted of, but it was a start.

"Everything okay?" Grayson asked.

She nodded. "They'd like you to stop by tomorrow and give them a statement."

He didn't say anything as he turned to stare out the window as they approached the palace gates. She chose to take his silence as a good sign, but she couldn't help but worry just a bit about the impression he'd gotten of Mirraccino. She could only hope the financial projections packet she'd put together would outweigh everything else.

Annabelle sat in the back of her sedan with Grayson as Berto ushered them past the security gates and onto the royal grounds. Annabelle had to admit that after living here for the past couple of years she'd begun to take the palace's beauty for granted.

She turned to Grayson to find him staring out the window. He seemed to be taking in the manicured lawns, the towering palm trees and the red-and-white border of flowers lining the long and winding drive.

"This place is remarkable." Grayson said, drawing her from her thoughts. "We have nothing like this where I come from."

"You're from California, right?"

He nodded, but he never took his gaze off the colorful scenery. "I couldn't even imagine what it must be like to live here."

"You get used to it." As strange as that might sound, this big place felt like home to her. "Is this your first visit to Mirraccino?"

"Yes." He still didn't look at her.

The turrets of the palace were first to come into view. They were colorful with stripes of yellow, pink, aqua and gold. Annabelle found herself looking at them through new eyes.

And then the palace in its entirety loomed. It

was enormous, even compared to her family's spacious mansion back in Halencia. While her home in Halencia was all white, the palace was created in warm shades of tan and coral with some accents done in aqua. It was simple and yet stunning.

And with the afternoon sun's rays, the palace practically gleamed. When she was a little girl, she'd thought the palace was magical. She'd always wanted to be a princess, but her mother assured her that she didn't need to be a princess to be special.

Being the daughter of the Duke of Halencia, she was addressed as Lady Annabelle. It gave her recognition in high society but not much else. Her father's estate would eventually revert to her older brother, the Earl of Halencia. She used to think it was unfair, but now she appreciated having choices in life.

The car pulled to a stop outside the palace. Berto rushed to get the car door. Annabelle alighted from the car followed by Grayson.

Grayson turned to her. "Why is the South Shore so important to you that you'd go out of your way for me?"

She schooled her features, trying to hide any hint of her desperation. "The South Shore was a pet project of the crown prince. He brought me in on the project at the beginning. When his responsibilities drew him away, I promised to see that it was finished."

"So you're keeping a promise to the prince?" Grayson arched a brow.

"He's my friend as well as my cousin," she was quick to clarify.

"That's right. You did mention the king was your uncle. So this is a family favor of sorts?"

"Yes. You could put it that way." If that's what he wanted to believe, who was she to change his mind? Because in the beginning that's all it had been. Now it was her way to prove herself to her father. "But in the process, I've really come to care about the people of the South Shore and I want to see it flourish."

He smiled at her, making her stomach quiver with the sensation of butterflies. "In that case, lead the way."

She didn't normally enter through the main door, but Grayson was a special guest—pivotal to her future. It wouldn't hurt to give him the VIP treatment.

Berto swung open the enormous wooden door with the large brass handle. They stepped inside the palace and once again she consciously surveyed her surroundings from the marble floor of the grand entryway to the high ceiling with the crystal chandelier suspended in the center. As a little girl, when there was a royal ball, she'd sneak down here and dance around the table in the center of the floor. She'd pretend that she truly was a princess attending the ball. Oh, the silly things kids did.

Grayson took in the opulent room. "I couldn't even imagine what it must be like to live here."

She shrugged. "It has its protocols and a system that it's best not to tamper with, but other than that I imagine it's like most other homes."

Grayson laughed. "I don't think so."

Just then, Alfred, the butler, came rushing into the room. "Lady Annabelle, I'm sorry. I didn't hear you arrive."

"No problem. I was just showing Mr. Landers around."

The butler gave her guest a discerning once-over. "Yes, ma'am. Is there anything I can do for you?"

"No, thanks. I was just going to show Mr. Landers to his suite of rooms so he can freshen up. Could you let the kitchen know that there will be one more for dinner?"

"Yes, ma'am. Shall I inform the king?"

Normally, she would say yes, but seeing as Grayson was a special guest who could make such a difference to her future, she said, "I'll speak to my uncle. Thank you."

Annabelle showed Grayson to the sweeping steps to the upstairs. A comfortable silence engulfed them as Grayson continued to take in his surroundings. She had to admit the palace was a lot more like a museum than a home. There were so many priceless works of art and gifts from other nations.

But more than anything, she wondered what thoughts were going through Grayson's mind. There was so much she wanted to know about him. As her uncle said often, knowledge was power. And she needed the power to push through this business deal.

She tried to tell herself that was the only reason she wanted to know more about Grayson. After all, it had nothing to do with his good looks or the way he was able to connect with her back at the piazza.

No. It was none of those things. It was purely business.

CHAPTER FOUR

Okay. So maybe this isn't so bad.

A vacation in a Mediterranean palace.

In fact, the palace is the perfect inspiration for a new game for Fo Shizzle.

Grayson sat in the formal dining room at a very large table. Did they really eat here every day? He might be rich, but he'd come from a humble beginning. He didn't stand on airs and most of the time his dinner was eaten alone in front of his desktop computer.

Meeting the king had been a great honor. Thankfully Annabelle had instructed him on the proper protocol while they were in the car. He wondered how he should have greeted her considering she was the daughter of a duke. He'd hazard a guess it wasn't to argue about what to do with her purse after the theft.

And try as he might, he couldn't help but like Annabelle. Not that he would let her sunny smiles get to him. He'd learned his lesson about love, especially about loving someone in the spotlight. And Annabelle, with her constant bodyguard, was definitely someone who was used to living in the spotlight—a place where he felt uncomfortable.

"Mr. Landers, you picked an optimal time to visit Mirraccino," the king said as their dinner dishes were cleared from the table.

How exactly did one make small talk with a king? Grayson swallowed hard. "Please call me Grayson." When the man nodded, Grayson continued. "If you don't mind me asking, why is this an optimal time?"

The king turned to Annabelle. "You didn't tell him about the heritage festival?"

"It slipped my mind." Color rushed to her cheeks. "I mean, there was so much going on this afternoon. I apologize. You are most definitely welcome to stay and partake in the festivities."

"No apology is necessary." Grayson could understand that the theft had shaken her up.

"Annabelle," the king said, "you need to slow down. I think you're becoming a workaholic."

Feeling bad for Annabelle, Grayson intervened. "I'd love to hear more about this heritage festival."

The king leaned back in his chair as the wait staff supplied them with coffee and a dessert plate of finger foods. "The heritage festival is an annual event. It's held in Portolina, which is a small village within walking distance of the palace. The villagers get together—actually people from all over the nation make the pilgrimage to Portolina for the four-day celebration."

Grayson took a sip of his coffee and then gently set it back on the fine china saucer which had tiny blue flowers around the edge. He didn't think he'd ever used such delicate dishes. With his big hands, he was afraid of touching such fragile items. He had no doubt that they were antiques. And he didn't even want to imagine their value. He might be wealthy, but there was a vast difference between his wealth and that of the king.

Grayson pulled his dessert plate closer. "I actually don't know if I'll be here that long."

The king picked up a mini pecan tart. "You really don't want to miss the event. Maybe you could extend your vacation. You would be my guest, here at the palace."

"Thank you, sir. I...I'll see if I can adjust my schedule."

"Good. You'll enjoy all of the activities." The king acted as though Grayson had said yes. The king added some sugar to his coffee and stirred. "You are here to determine if the South Shore is appropriate for your business. I hope you found it as beautiful as we do."

"I did, sir." That was certainly not one of the reasons he was hesitant to put in one of his cafés. But he really didn't want to get into the details with the king. "I'd like a chance to check into a few more locations before I commit my company. And as soon as this situation with Annabelle and the police is wrapped up—"

"Police?" The king sat up straight. A distinct frown marred his face as he turned to his niece. "Why is this the first I'm hearing of an incident with the police?"

Color flooded Annabelle's face. "It's not a big deal."

"I'll be the judge of that." The king turned back to Grayson. "What exactly happened?"

"Uncle, I'll explain." Annabelle sent Grayson a warning look. "There's no need to drag Grayson into this."

"It appears he's already a part of it. He at least knows what happened, which is more than I do." The King turned back to him and gestured for Grayson to spill the details.

Grayson swallowed hard. "It really isn't that big of a deal."

"If it involves my niece, it's a very big deal."

Grayson glanced down at the small plate filled with sweets. He suddenly lost his appetite. He launched into the details of his first meeting with Annabelle. He tried to downplay the events, realizing how much the king worried about her. And Grayson knew what happened when a high-profile person didn't heed safety protocols.

When Grayson finished reciting the events as best as he could recall them, the king gestured for the phone. He announced that he was going to speak with the police.

"Uncle, I have everything under control."

The man sent her a pointed look. "It doesn't sound like it. You don't have your purse and you don't know what's going to happen to that thief." He shook his head as he accepted the phone that had already been dialed for him. "What is this world coming to when you can't even walk down the street without being accosted?"

"Uncle, it was nothing. I don't know who is worse. You, or my father?"

"We just want you to be safe." The king pressed the phone to his ear and began talking.

Grayson found the whole dynamic between these two quite interesting. They were comfortable enough with each other even though they were in opposition. Annabelle was noticeably seething under all of the fuss, but she restrained her emotions. And her uncle looked worried. These two obviously loved each other deeply.

The king didn't say much during the phone conversation. It seemed as if he was getting a blow-by-blow explanation of the chain of events. Grayson glanced at Annabelle, who looked miserable. He was sorry that he'd opened his mouth. He had thought the king would have been informed. After all, Annabelle was his niece.

"There. That's resolved," the king said as he disconnected the call. "You and Grayson are to go to the police station tomorrow morning. They will be expecting you. Grayson needs to give his statement, as do you. As for your belongings, they should be able to give you your wallet but the rest is evidence."

"I know," Annabelle said.

The king's eyes widened. "What do you mean, you know?"

"I'd already called and made arrangements to go to the station in the morning."

For a moment her uncle didn't say a word and neither did anyone else.

Finally, the king got to his feet. "Now, if you'll excuse me. I am needed elsewhere."

Grayson didn't know whether to stand or remain

seated. When Annabelle stood, he followed her lead. They didn't sit back down until the king was out of sight. Once seated again, Grayson took a sip of coffee and waited until Annabelle was ready to speak.

"I'm sorry about that," she said while staring at her coffee cup.

"It's no big deal."

"But you didn't come here to witness some family drama."

"It's okay. I understand." Grayson didn't. Not really. His parents lived in rural Ohio and were so caught up in their own lives that they never gave him a second thought. He didn't know what it was like to have your every move under a microscope. He imagined that it would be quite oppressive.

"No, you don't," Annabelle said wearily. "My life…it's complicated."

If he were smart, he'd get to his feet and head for his suite. They'd done enough sharing for one day, but he couldn't turn his back on her. She obviously needed someone to lend her an ear.

He cleared his throat while searching for some words of comfort. "Everyone's life is complicated. It's how you get through it all that matters."

She arched a fine brow. "Even yours?"

He nodded. "Even mine."

"But you're rich and you run your own company. You don't have people telling you what to do and thinking they know better. You get to call all of the shots."

Grayson laughed. "If that's what you think, then you've got it all wrong. My name may be on the company letterhead, but I have a board and share-holders to answer to. A lot of those shareholders think they have all of the answers, even though they are far removed from our target clientele and know nothing about our product and its design."

"Oh. I didn't realize." She paused as though letting this information sink in. "But you only have to deal with it as far as your business is con-cerned. At least, they aren't involved in your per-sonal life."

Grayson rubbed the back of his neck. Now she was heading into exceedingly uncomfortable ter-ritory. Time for a change of subjects. "Should we go to the police station together in the morning?"

"After what happened with my uncle, I didn't think you'd want anything to do with me."

"Seriously? That was nothing. Trust me, my fa-ther ruined more dinners than I could ever count. What your uncle did was just his way of showing that he cares about you and is worried about your safety."

Her eyes widened with surprise. "You really believe that? Or are you just trying to make me feel better?"

He wasn't going to feed her a line. Other people had done that to him and he knew it wasn't helpful. "How about a little of both?"

A small smile pulled at her lips. "Thanks for being honest. I really appreciate it."

"You're welcome."

She studied him for a moment, making him a little uncomfortable.

"Do I have something on my mouth?" When she shook her head, he asked, "My nose? My chin?" She continued to shake her head but a smile had started to lift her lips. "Then what is it?"

"You look tired. Is it jet lag?"

"Actually, it is. I can't sleep on planes." He always envied those people who could snooze after takeoff and wake up at landing.

Annabelle got to her feet. "Why don't we call it an evening?"

"But the financials?"

"Can wait until tomorrow." She started for the door and he followed.

It wasn't until she paused outside his room that he realized she hadn't answered his question. "About the police station—"

"Oh, yes. We can go together. Is first thing in the morning all right?"

"It's fine with me. Just ignore the jet lag."

Then hesitantly she asked, "Will it be a problem if my bodyguard accompanies us?"

"Not a problem at all." A question came to his mind although he wasn't sure if he should ask, but seeing as they were starting to open up to each other, he decided to go with it. "Are you always under protection?"

"Yes. Ever since my mother was murdered."

"Murdered?"

Annabelle averted her gaze and nodded. It was obviously still painful for her. He couldn't even imagine the pain she'd been living with.

Grayson cleared his throat. "I'm sorry."

Her gaze finally met his. "Thank you."

"Your father, he thinks the person is going to come after you? After all of this time?"

"I don't know what he thinks. The official report says that she died during a mugging. My father doesn't believe it, but he has no proof of anything to the contrary. And it isn't just me that my father has a protective detail on. It's my brother too. But Luca doesn't let it bother him. He still keeps up with his globe-trotting, partying ways. Maybe that's his way of dealing with everything. I don't know. We've grown apart over the years."

"I take it you don't believe your father's suspicions?"

"Quite honestly, today is the first time he's shared this information with me. And I don't know what to make of it."

"So your brother doesn't know?"

She shook her head. "I wouldn't even know what to tell him."

The look in her eyes told Grayson this was all very troubling for her. It was best to change the subject. "I always wanted a brother or sister, but fate had other ideas. And now looking back on things, I guess it was for the best. They were spared."

"Your home life was that bad?" She pressed her lips together as though realizing she was being nosey. "Sorry. I shouldn't have asked."

"It's okay. I started this conversation. As for my family, we saw things differently. My father grew up working with his hands, tilling the ground and planting seeds. I was never interested in that sort of life and it infuriated him. He thought I should do the same as he'd done and follow in the family tradition of farming." Grayson shifted his weight from one foot to the other. "Let's just say those discussions became heated."

"And your mother?"

"She always sided with my father. They were always so worried about what I should be doing with my life that they never stopped and asked what I wanted to do with it."

"I'm sorry. That's tough. But somehow you overcame it all and made yourself into a success."

"Trust me. It wasn't easy. And I wouldn't want to do it again."

"Do you still speak with your parents?"

"I haven't seen them in years. When I walked out, my father told me that if I left I would never be welcome again. I guess he meant it because I've never heard from them."

"That's so sad."

"The reason I told you that is because I don't want to see the same thing happen with you and your family."

"But this is different—"

"Not that much. You are struggling for your freedom and they are struggling to keep you safe. You can't both have your own way. Someone is going to win this struggle and someone is going to lose. The key is not to destroy your relationship in the process."

"You sound so wise for someone so young."

"I don't know about that. Maybe I just wish someone had given me some advice along the way instead of me always having to learn things the hard way."

"Well, don't worry. Things are about to change." She pressed her lips together and glanced away as though she'd just realized she'd said too much.

"Ah, you have a plan."

"It's nothing. I should be going. I've forgotten to give the king a message from my father." And with that she rushed off down the hallway.

Grayson watched her go. He couldn't help but wonder about this plan of hers and if it was going to get her into trouble. It was obvious that she wasn't ready to share the details with him. But that didn't keep him from worrying about this *plan*. His mind told him it was absolutely none of his business, but his gut told him that she might get herself into trouble trying to prove a point.

And he might have just met her, but he already realized she was stubborn. Stubborn enough not to ask for help? But what was he supposed to do about any of it?

CHAPTER FIVE

ALONE AT LAST.

The next morning, Annabelle hurried to her suite of rooms as soon as she'd returned from the police station. Grayson had stayed behind in Bellacitta to meet with a business associate. They'd agreed to meet up later to go over the financial projections for the South Shore Project.

She'd been relieved to have a little time to herself. At last, she'd recovered her mother's journal, and she had some privacy to look at it. And if she'd had any qualms about invading her mother's privacy, the police had remedied them. They had her open the journal and read just a bit to herself to verify it belonged to her. She didn't correct their assumption that it was her journal.

Alone in her room, Annabelle sat down at her desk in front of the window that overlooked the blue waters of the Mediterranean. And though usually she took solace in the majestic view, today her thoughts were elsewhere.

As the hours ticked by, she turned page after page. There were old snapshots stuffed between the pages. Some of her mother and father. Some of Annabelle and her brother. There was so much history crammed between the leather covers that it floored her.

And thankfully, there was nothing scandalous or cringeworthy within the pages. Not even anything blushworthy lurked in the passages, which was a gigantic relief to Annabelle. It was almost as if her mother had known that one day one of her children would be reading it.

Instead, the journal read more like the highlights of a royal's life. There were mentions of birthday celebrations, picnics, holidays and countless other events that Annabelle had either been too young to remember or hadn't bothered to really notice. But her mother had remembered and made note of colorful details that brought the passages to life. And it had been a nice life, not perfect, but the bad times were smoothed over and the good times highlighted. That's how she remembered her mother—always trying to fix things and make people smile.

Annabelle didn't even notice lunchtime coming or going. At some point, she moved from the desk chair to the comfort of her big canopied bed with its array of silken pillows. She couldn't remember the last time she'd curled up in bed with a book in the middle of the day. It felt so decadent. She continued devouring word after word, feeling closer to her mother than she'd felt in a very long time.

Knock. Knock.

Annabelle's gaze jerked to the door, expecting one of the household staff to enter with fresh flowers or clean linens. A frown pulled at her lips. She really didn't want to be disturbed. She still had a lot of pages to read.

Knock. Knock.

"Annabelle? Is everything okay?"

It was Grayson. And something told her he wasn't going to leave until they spoke. With a sigh, she closed the journal and set it off to the side of the bed. Hating to leave her comfy spot, she grudgingly got to her feet.

She moved to the door and then paused to run a hand over her hair. Deciding that it was good enough, she reached for the doorknob.

"Hi." She couldn't help but stare at his handsome face and piercing blue eyes. Now that he'd shaved, his looks were a perfect ten.

He frowned. "Why do you keep looking at me that way?"

"What way?" She averted her gaze. She was

going to have to be more covert with her admiration in the future.

He sighed. "Never mind."

She stepped back, allowing him to enter the room. "Come in."

He stepped into her spacious suite and glanced around. She followed his gaze around the room, taking in the settee, the armchairs, a table with a bouquet of flowers and her desk. She noticed how his gaze lingered on the king-size bed.

At last, his gaze met hers. "You missed lunch?"

"Did we have plans?" She didn't recall any. In fact, Grayson had said he planned to remain in the city for most of the day.

"No, we didn't. But I wrapped up my meeting early and returned to the palace. I thought I would see you at lunch and when you didn't show up, I...I just wanted to make sure everything was all right."

"Oh, yes, everything is fine. I was reading." She gestured toward the now rumpled bed.

Grayson's gaze followed her hand gesture. "It looks like I must have startled you."

"What?"

He moved toward the bed where he knelt down and picked up the journal from the floor. But that wasn't the only thing on the floor. The precious pictures were scattered about.

"Oh, no." She rushed over.

"No worries. Nothing's ruined."

"You don't have to pick that up," Annabelle said, kneeling down next to him. "I can get it."

"I don't mind." He picked up a photograph and glanced at it. "Is this you as a child?"

She looked at the photo and a rush of memories came back to her. "Yes. That's me and my brother, Luca."

"You were a cute kid."

"Thanks. I think." Her stomach quivered as Grayson's gaze lingered longer than necessary. She swallowed hard. "I can't believe my mother kept all of those pictures stuffed in her journal."

"Ah...so that's your mother's. It explains why you're so protective of it. I thought you were going to jump across that desk at the police station when the officer said he couldn't release it to you."

Heat rushed up Annabelle's neck and settled in her cheeks as she realized how that incident must have looked to others. But she'd been desperate to hang on to this link to her mother. And by reading the pages, she already felt as though she knew her mother so much better.

"Thanks for stepping up and reasoning with the officer," Annabelle said. "I just couldn't get him to understand my urgency."

"You're welcome."

"You know, you're not such a bad guy to have around."

His voice grew deep and gentle. "Is that your way of saying you'd like me to stay for the heritage festival?"

"Maybe." Did her voice sound as breathless to him as it did to her?

His head lifted and their gazes met. There was something different about the way he looked at her. And then it struck her with the force of an electrical surge—there was desire reflected in his gaze. He wanted her.

It was like a switch had been turned on and she was fully aware of the attraction arcing between them. Annabelle had never felt anything so vital and stirring with anyone else in her life. Maybe she'd led a more sheltered life than she'd ever imagined. Sure there had been other men, but those relationships had never had this sort of spark and soon they fizzled out.

With them kneeling down on the floor side by side, their faces were only mere inches apart. Did he have any idea what his close proximity did to her heart rate, not to mention her common sense?

His gaze dipped to her mouth and the breath

hitched in her throat. Was he going to kiss her? And was it wrong that she wanted him to?

Not waiting for him to make up his mind, she leaned forward, pressing her lips to his. If this was too bold, she didn't care. She'd been cautious all of her life, while her brother had been reckless. If she wanted things to change, then *she* had to change them, by taking more chances.

His lips were smooth and warm. Yet, he was hesitant. His mouth didn't move against hers. Oh, no! Had she read everything wrong?

Her problem was her lack of experience. She hadn't gotten out enough. She didn't know how to read men. Here she'd been thinking that he desired her and the thought had probably never crossed his mind. She was such a fool.

She started to pull back when his hand reached up, cupping her cheek. Her heart jumped into her throat. Then again, maybe she had been right. As he deepened the kiss, her heart thump-thumped. He did want her. And she most definitely wanted him.

Her hands slid up over his muscled shoulders and wrapped around the back of his neck. All the while, his thumb stroked her cheek, sending the most delicious sensations to her very core, heating it up and melting it down.

She didn't know where this was headed and she didn't care. The only thing that mattered was the here and now. And the here and now was quite delicious. Quite addictive—

Footsteps echoed in the hallway. Annabelle recalled leaving the door wide open.

She yanked back. Grayson let her go. It was as though they both realized that what was happening here wasn't practical. They came from different worlds and worse yet, they were involved in a business deal. She couldn't lose her focus.

Annabelle averted her gaze as she ran a shaky hand over her now tender lips. How could she face him again after she'd initiated that kiss—that soul-stirring kiss?

She glanced down at the mess still on the floor. Focus on anything but how good that kiss had been. Annabelle began picking up the papers when there was a knock at the door. She glanced up. "Come in."

A member of her uncle's staff appeared, holding a tray of food. "Excuse me, ma'am. The king asked that this tray be brought to you since you missed lunch."

"Oh. Thank you." She forced a smile. "You can leave it on the desk."

"Yes, ma'am." The young woman deposited the heavily laden tray and then turned for the door.

The door snicked shut as Annabelle turned back to Grayson. He was picking up the last of the photos and papers. They were now sorted into two piles. One of snapshots and one of scraps of papers.

"I think I got it all," Grayson said but his gaze never quite met hers.

So he regretted what just happened between them. She couldn't blame him. She'd let the attraction she'd felt since she first met him get the better of her. Now, she had to somehow repair the damage if she had any hope of getting him to bring his state-of-the-art gaming café to Mirraccino. And it wasn't just the café Grayson would bring to the area, but it would also be the headquarters for the Mediterranean arm of his business—an employment opportunity that would help Mirraccino.

"I'm sorry." They both said in unison.

The combined apology broke the tension. They both smiled—genuine smiles. Maybe this situation wasn't beyond repair after all. A girl could hope, couldn't she?

"I shouldn't have kissed you," Annabelle confessed.

"You didn't do it alone."

"But still, I initiated it. This is all on me."

He arched a brow. "I don't think so. I could have stopped you…if I'd wanted to."

Had she heard him correctly? Or was she just hearing what she wished to? "Are…are you saying you didn't want it to stop?"

His gaze searched hers. "If we're to continue to do business together that probably shouldn't happen again."

"Agreed." She averted her gaze. "And I think you're going to be impressed with the incentives we're willing to offer you to bring your business to Mirraccino."

"I'm looking forward to seeing the package."

As Annabelle continued to gaze down at the Oriental rug covering the wood floor, she noticed a cream-colored slip of paper sticking out from the edge of the bed. It must have come from the journal. She bent over and picked it up.

"Sorry," Grayson said. "I must have missed that one."

"It was most of the way under the bed. It's no wonder you missed it."

Wanting something to distract her from the jumble of emotions over Grayson's pending departure, she unfolded the slip of paper. Inside was a message. A very strange message.

"What's the matter?" Grayson asked.

"It's this note. It seems odd. Why would my mother have a note addressed to Cosmo? I don't even know any Cosmo."

"Do you mind if I take a look?"

There certainly wasn't anything personal in the note so she handed it over. It honestly didn't mean anything to her. Why in the world had her mother kept it? And why would she have placed it with her most sacred papers?

Grayson read the note aloud:

Cosmo, tea is my Gold. I drink it first in the morning and at four in the afternoon.

for you. I hope you enjOy. Am hopiNg The Queen Is weLL. Visit heR oftEn? Nate is Well. yOu muSt see Sara. She's growN very much. Everything is As you requesTed. Don't terry. Get goin noW. WishIng you all of tHe best.

"What do you make of it?" Annabelle asked.

Grayson stood up and turned the paper over as though searching for more clues as to why her mother had kept it. "You're sure it doesn't strike any chords in your memory?"

"None at all. In fact, can I see it again?" Annabelle examined the handwriting. "That's not even my mother's handwriting."

"That's odd. You're sure?"

"Positive." She moved to the bed and retrieved her mother's journal and flipped it open to a random page. "See. Very different handwriting."

"I have to agree with you. Perhaps it wasn't in the journal. Maybe someone who stayed here before you dropped it."

"Impossible. I've been in this room for a couple of years and trust me when I say they clean the palace from top to bottom without missing a thing. No, this had to have come from the journal. But my question is why did my mother keep such a cryptic note?"

Grayson backed away. "I can't help you with that."

She folded the note and slipped it back in the journal. It was just one more mystery where her mother was concerned. Annabelle would try to figure it out, but later. Right now, she had to convince Grayson that Mirraccino was a good fit for Fo Shizzle.

"We should go over those financial projections now." She glanced at him, hoping he'd be agreeable. "Unless you have other plans."

He shook his head. "I'm all yours."

His words set her stomach aquiver with nervous energy. She knew he'd meant nothing intimate by the words, but it didn't stop her mind from wondering *what if*?

* * *

A couple of hours later, Annabelle stared across the antique mahogany table in the library at Grayson. She'd successfully answered all of his questions about the financial projections and the future of the South Shore.

He was still reading over the material. There was a lot of it. She'd worked hard to present a thorough package. But she had one other idea up her sleeve.

Grayson straightened the papers and slid them back in the folder. "You've certainly given me a lot to think about. Between the proposed national advertising campaign and the tax reduction, I'm impressed."

"Good." But he still didn't seem thoroughly convinced and that worried her.

He picked up the folder. "I appreciate your thoroughness."

She refused to stop while she was on a roll. If she could bring this deal about, the South Shore would have an amazing facility for seniors in need of assistance. It would have decent-priced housing for young families. And this café would give young people a reason to hang out in the South Shore without causing a ruckus. And from the reviews she'd read about the cafés in other cities, it would provide a popular tourist destination.

"Why not hang out with me today?" she asked in her best cajoling voice. When his gaze narrowed in on her, she smiled.

"I have some reports to review and emails to answer."

"Can't they wait just a little bit?" She had to think fast here. "After all, it's a beautiful day in Mirraccino. And this is your first and perhaps your last trip here. And you haven't seen that much of the island."

"I've seen enough—"

"To know that it's beautiful. But I haven't yet shown you other parts of it. Mirraccino is a complex nation. It has a rich history, but it is also a thriving community with a technology base that tops the region. And there are lots of young people—young people who would like the opportunity to remain here in Mirraccino when they complete their education."

Grayson rubbed a hand over his clean-shaven jaw. "I don't know."

The way his eyes twinkled told her he was playing with her. She asked, "Are you going to make me beg?"

Surprise and interest lit up his handsome face. "I—think—"

"You'll be a gentleman and accept my invitation without making me go to such great extremes."

He smiled and shook his head. "Boy, you know how to take the fun out of things."

"I thought fun was what we just had before we were interrupted." She was blatantly flirting with him, something she rarely did, but there was something about him—something that brought out the impish side of her.

"Is that what we were doing?"

He wanted her. It was written all over his face and as much as she'd like to fall into his arms, they'd both agreed it wasn't a good idea. There was work to be done. And she wasn't about to confuse her priorities again.

Before lunch, she'd had the forethought to set up some appointments at the university with the faculty and some of the computer science students. She had a feeling if he were to see this island nation for all of its benefits, he'd change his mind about expanding his business here. At least she hoped…

And what was in it for her? Besides helping her community once their business was concluded, she wouldn't mind another of those mind-blowing kisses. Not that she was anxious for anything serious. She didn't have time for a relationship. But if he were to set up a business in Mirraccino, she might be able to make time for a little fun. As it was, all work and no play made for a dull Annabelle. That's what her brother always used to tell her. Maybe he wasn't all wrong.

Grayson quietly studied her for a moment. "Okay. You've won me over. Let's go."

Yay! This plan would work. She knew what he wanted and now she could show him that Mirraccino could provide it. "Just give me a second to freshen up."

"Do you mind if I take another look at that cryptic note?"

His question surprised her, but she didn't see how it would hurt. While Grayson read over the note, Annabelle touched up her makeup and swept her hair up into a ponytail. She knew that it was fine just the way it was, but she had an impulse to look her best. Not that she was trying to impress anyone of course…

CHAPTER SIX

"WELL?"

Grayson couldn't help but smile at Annabelle's enthusiasm. Her eyes twinkled when she was excited and she couldn't stand still. She stared at him with rapt attention.

"It'd been a long time since someone had looked at him like he was at the center of their world. He'd forgotten how good it felt for someone to care about his opinion. Was it wrong that he didn't want it to end?

"Grayson, please, say something."

"I really enjoyed today. Thank you."

Her smile broadened and puffed up her cheeks. She was adorable. And a business associate—nothing more. It was for the best. "How much?"

"How much what?"

"How much did you enjoy today?" She clasped her hands together. "Enough to seriously consider Mirraccino for your new headquarters?"

He couldn't help but laugh at her eagerness. "How could I say no to that pleading look?"

"You mean it?"

He nodded. What he didn't tell her was that he'd made up his mind after reviewing the financial package. "I sent the figures to my team to consider."

"I knew you'd like it here."

Grayson began walking along the sidewalk of the great Mirraccino Royal University with Annabelle by his side. He didn't say things that he didn't mean. And he wasn't truly impressed that often, but today he had been.

He was glad that he'd relented and decided to give Annabelle...erm... Mirraccino another try. Annabelle had arranged for a most impressive tour of the up-to-date campus. He'd talked with the professors in the computer science department. And he'd even agreed to give a spontaneous guest lecture.

To his relief, the lecture had gone well and the students had been quite receptive to his talk on his company's cloud technology and how they'd harnessed it to make their café games relevant and constantly morphing into something bigger and better.

"Really? You were honestly impressed?" Annabelle came to a stop in front of him. Hope reflected in her eyes.

"Yes, I meant it. Why do you sound so surprised?"

"I don't know. I'm not. It's just—"

"You weren't so sure about today, were you?"

She shrugged. "Not really. I wanted to believe you'd see the full potential that Mirraccino could offer you—offer your company, but yesterday you seemed to have made your mind up about everything."

He couldn't let her stop there. "And what have I decided about you?"

Annabelle glanced away. "That I'm spoiled and overprotected."

"That isn't what I think. That is what *you* think, but it shouldn't be. I think you work hard for what you want. Setting up everything today couldn't have been easy, especially when it was done at the last minute."

Her gaze met his. "I called in every favor I had here at the school. But to be honest, when I spoke to the head of the computer science department and told him who I wanted to bring for a visit, he was more than willing to help. You have quite an amazing reputation in your field."

"I don't know about that, but I appreciate your kind words."

When she gazed deep into his eyes, like she was doing now, it was so hard to remember that they were supposed to be doing business together and not picking up that kiss where they'd left off. His gaze latched on to her tempting mouth. What would she say? His gaze moved back to her eyes. Was that desire he spied glinting within them?

He didn't know how long they stood there, staring into each other's eyes. In that moment, there was nowhere else he needed to be—nowhere else he wanted to be. There was a special quality about Annabelle that sparked life back into him. She filled in all the cracks in his heart and made him want to face whatever life threw at him.

A motion out of the corner of his eye reminded him they weren't alone. Today there was a female bodyguard escorting them. She was not the friendly sort—always on guard. He recalled Annabelle calling the woman Marta.

Having a bodyguard watch over them dampened his lusty thoughts. He didn't like an audience and he preferred not to end up in one of those reports sent off to the Duke of Halencia. But that didn't mean their outing should end just yet.

"How about we go to dinner? I'd enjoy trying one of the local restaurants."

Surprise lit up Annabelle's eyes, but in a blink her enthusiasm dimmed. "Um, sure."

"What's the matter?"

"Why does anything need to be the matter?"

"Because it was written all over your face and it was in your tone."

"It's nothing. You're just imagining things." She glanced away and pulled out her phone. "I know the perfect spot. I'll just call ahead and let them know we're on our way."

He didn't believe her protests. There was something weighing on her mind, but he didn't push the subject. If she wanted to confide in him, she would have to do it of her own accord. Once she made the call, they started across the campus toward the parking lot.

After touring this university with its state-of-the-art facilities and cutting-edge technology, he realized there was a lot more to this island nation than its obvious beauty and rich history. The university was surprisingly large, drawing students from all over Europe and there were even some Americans in the mix.

There was a wealth of knowledge here. Some of the students had heard of his cafés and had pleaded with him to build one in Mirraccino. And there were other students who were anxious to work for him.

It would mean his company wouldn't have to go outside Mirraccino every time they needed to hire personnel for the technological portion of the business. And with some combined initiatives with the university, word about the café would reach the targeted demographic.

"What has you so quiet?" Annabelle asked, interrupting his thoughts.

"I was just going over the events of the day."

"I'm glad you enjoyed your visit. You know, I graduated from this university with a business degree. I never knew what I'd do with it, but the South Shore Project has been good for me. I like getting up in the morning and having a purpose. Too bad the project is winding down."

"Then why don't you find another job?"

She shrugged. "It's hard to have a normal job when you have someone shadowing your every move."

"Maybe your circumstances will change and you'll be able to do as you please."

Annabelle lowered her voice. "That's my plan."

Again the warning bells went off in his mind. He couldn't resist asking, "What plan?"

She glanced over her shoulder as though making certain her bodyguard wasn't within earshot. "I plan to show my father that I'm fully capable of caring for myself and that he no longer has to watch over me. And when you sign on with the South Shore, he'll have to acknowledge that fact."

"And if your father doesn't agree? Then what?"

"Then I'm leaving. I've always wanted to travel. Maybe I'll go to London, Paris," she paused and stared at him, "or perhaps I'll go to California."

He didn't believe she'd actually do it. "Could you really walk away from your father and uncle?"

"Why not?" she said with bravado. "It'll make their lives easier. After all, you left your family. Why shouldn't I?"

"My circumstances were different." There was no comparison between their situations. He had to make her understand. "Your father and uncle love you very much. That's why they worry so much. I never had anyone worry about me."

"I'm sorry. I… I shouldn't have said anything."

He couldn't leave off there. He had to stop her from making a big mistake. "When I left, my parents didn't try to stop me. When I rejected their way of life, I became dead to them. But if you leave here, your father and uncle will never stop looking for you."

"So they can stick their security detail on me—"

"No, because they love you and your absence would make them sad. Please tell me you understand what a gift you have here."

"I...I do." She twisted her purse strap around her fingers. "But somewhere along the way that love started to smother me. My father doesn't accept that my mother has been dead for eleven years and if there were any lingering dangers, something would have happened by now."

He sure hoped she was right. Still, there was an uneasy feeling in his gut. But then again he probably wasn't the best judge of danger. His thoughts strayed back to his last girlfriend. A harmless day of fun had turned deadly. And he'd missed all of the signs. So maybe he was just being overly sensitive now.

They rounded the corner of the administration office when a group of reporters rushed them. Grayson's whole body tensed. He'd known this moment would come sooner or later. He'd been hoping for later.

Annabelle's bodyguard rushed in front of them, waving off the paparazzi.

Members of the press started yelling out questions. "Lady Annabelle, is it true? Do you have a new love interest?"

"Does the king approve?"

"How long have you two been involved?"

The questions kept coming one after the other in rapid succession. Thanks to social media, they couldn't even visit the university without the whole world knowing.

He glanced over at Annabelle and was surprised to find her keeping it all together. But then again as a member of the royal family, she was probably used to these occurrences. Now he better understood her father's reluctance to lift the security detail.

Campus security quickly responded. Grayson guessed that the bodyguard had alerted them. With help, they made it to their car. Marta drove as he sat with Annabelle in the backseat. But when they took off out of the parking lot, they were followed.

As their speed increased so did Grayson's anxiety. His fingers bit into the door handle. His body tensed as memories washed over him. Usually he only visited this nightmare when it was late and he was alone. But now it was happening right before his wide-open eyes.

His past and present collided. He recalled the moments leading up to the hideous chain of events. It was like a horror movie playing in his mind and he was helpless to stop it.

"Grayson, are you okay?" Annabelle asked.

He nodded, not trusting his voice at that moment.

"No, you're not." She pressed a hand to his cheek. "You feel okay, but you're pale as a ghost."

"I'm fine," he ground out.

Just then there was a bang. He jumped, nearly hitting his head on the roof. In the next instant, he was leaning over to Annabelle and pulling her as close as possible with seat belt restraints still on.

"Grayson, let me up." She pushed on his chest.

He hesitated. Not hearing any further gunfire, he moved, allowing Annabelle to sit fully upright.

"What was that?" she asked, uneasiness filling her voice.

Grayson didn't dare say what he thought it was. He didn't want to scare her any more than necessary. Sadly, he knew what a gunshot sounded like from inside a vehicle.

"A vehicle backfired," Marta said from the driver's seat.

Annabelle's hand slipped in his and squeezed.

A backfire? That knowledge should make him feel better and put him at ease, but it didn't. There were still paparazzi in cars and motorcycles swarming all around them. Their chaotic and unwanted caravan was flying down the highway now.

"Marta, take us back to the palace," Annabelle ordered.

The bodyguard never took her gaze off the road. "Understood. I'll let the palace know we're coming in hot."

Annabelle leaned her head against Grayson's shoulder. "I'm so sorry. Don't worry. We'll be at the palace soon."

"I'm fine." Why did he keep saying that? He was anything but fine. It was just that he wasn't ready to open up about his past. He didn't want to see the disappointment in Annabelle's eyes when she knew that he wasn't such a great guy after all.

"No, you're not. If it's the paparazzi, I'm sorry. I guess I didn't think about them getting wind of us being at the university. But I'm sure some of the students got excited and were posting pictures and messages about the visit on their social media accounts."

They remained hand in hand the rest of the way back to the palace where there was a heavy contingent of armed guards. There was no way any reporter was going to get past the gates.

As the gates swung closed behind them and their speed drastically reduced, Grayson could at last take a full breath. He felt foolish for letting the incident affect him so greatly. It'd been a while since he'd had a panic attack. There'd been a period after the accident when he'd stopped leaving his Malibu beach house for this very reason.

It'd been more than a year since the accident. He'd thought that he would have been past it by now. But the idea of the same thing happening to Annabelle shook him to the core.

When the vehicle pulled to a stop in front of the palace, he immediately jumped out. He'd made an utter fool of himself. How could he not tell the difference between a gunshot and a car backfiring? What was the matter with him?

He needed some fresh air and a chance to pull himself together before he faced Annabelle's inevitable questions. He couldn't blame her for wondering what was going on with him, but he didn't know what to tell her. He'd never discussed that very painful episode with anyone but a counselor. And he wasn't going to start now.

He took off in the direction of the beach. He knew from talking to Annabelle that it was private. He would be safe from prying eyes there.

"Grayson, wait," Annabelle called out.

He kept moving.

"Let him go," Marta said.

"But he…" Annabelle's voice faded into the breeze.

The more he walked, the calmer he got. And his jumbled thoughts smoothed out. Needing a diversion, he pondered the strange note that Annabelle had found among her mother's things. There was something about the message that continued to nag at him.

He pulled his phone from his pocket. On it was an image of the note. He'd taken the photo because his gut was telling him there was something about it that wasn't quite right. But what was it?

He read the note once, then twice and a third time. Was it the misspelled words that bothered him? Or perhaps the mix of lowercase and uppercase letters? Or was it the fact the message just didn't say much of anything?

Who in the world would write such a cryptic note?

And why would Annabelle's mother place it in her journal?

There was more going on here than they knew. But what was it?

CHAPTER SEVEN

THIS WAS HER FAULT.

Annabelle felt horrible about the paparazzi's appearance at the university and the ensuing chase. Though Grayson was a multimillionaire and famous, he didn't appear used to the hounding press.

She hadn't thought of that aspect when she'd made arrangements to take him there. She'd been so anxious to show him how well his business would fit in here that she hadn't taken time to plan a rear exit from the campus to avoid the press.

If it hadn't been for Grayson's adverse reaction, she might have turned the situation around and given a public statement about the pending contract with the Fo Shizzle Café chain. But on second thought, she would have been rushing things. There was no verbal or paper contract...yet.

And after today, there might not be one. Unless she could turn things around. First, she needed to get the press off their trail. And then she needed to smooth things over with Grayson.

She called the palace's press secretary and set up a brief statement to be given just outside the palace gates where the paparazzi were lying in wait. She knew from past experience that they wouldn't go away until they got a story—whether it be the truth or a bit of fiction that they conjured up.

And next, she called the kitchen and requested a candlelit dinner to be served on the patio overlooking the sea. She didn't know if Grayson would be in any mood to join her, but she wanted to make the effort since their prior dinner plans had been ruined.

With all of the arrangements made, she put on a pair of dark jeans, a white blouse and a navy blazer. She piled her hair atop her head. She wore a modest amount of makeup and chose gold hoop earrings and a necklace to match. Simple and presentable.

Her stomach churned with nerves. She never liked talking with the press. Some would say that she should be used to it, being part of a royal family. But she was the same as everyone else and longed for a private life.

Knowing she had to do this if she wanted the press to lay off, she made her way down the grand staircase. In her mind, she went over and over what she would say to the reporters. It was her intention to give a statement and not accept questions because quite honestly, she wouldn't know how to answer any questions about her relationship with Grayson. It was very complicated to say the least.

This time not only was her bodyguard present, but a bunch of palace security met her in the grand foyer of the palace. And then she spied her uncle talking with the palace guards. She inwardly groaned.

Knowing there was no way to avoid the king, she walked directly toward him. "Hello, Uncle."

"Don't hello me. What's going on?" His voice grew husky with concern. "I heard there was a high-speed pursuit with the paparazzi today. You know that's dangerous. You should have used the protocols that we have in place if you are going to do something high profile."

"But it wasn't high profile. It was a visit to the university."

"The university?"

Annabelle explained what had led her and Grayson to the school. And she admitted to the fact that she hadn't anticipated the students making a big deal of the visit via social media. It was her slipup and no one else's.

The king nodded in understanding. "You have

to be careful. Your life is not like other peoples'. You must take precautions."

"You know, sometimes when you say that you sound just like my father."

"Well, that's because your father is right."

"Right or wrong, I have to go talk to the press."

"You could let the press secretary handle it. That's what we pay her to do."

Annabelle shook her head. "I started all of this and if there is to be any peace for the remainder of Grayson's stay, I must fix it."

Her uncle sighed. "You always were a stubborn girl. So much like your mother. Do what you must, but a full security team will accompany you."

She knew better than to argue with the king. There was only so much he was willing to concede and she knew she'd hit that limit. She was fine with the escort as long as they hung back.

She gave her uncle a hug. "I'm sorry I worried you. That was never my intention."

"I know. Though some may think otherwise, it's not always an easy life. There are limitations to what we can or should do."

"I understand. I will be more cautious."

And with her uncle's blessing she set off down the drive to address the media. Though her insides shivered with nervous energy, she kept moving.

She would fix this and then she would speak with Grayson.

The household knew to alert her when he returned from his walk. So far she hadn't heard a word. Surely he'd be back soon.

CHAPTER EIGHT

IT WAS A CIPHER.

Grayson picked up his pace as he retraced his footsteps back to the palace. The calming sound of the water and the gentle breeze had soothed his agitation as he'd hoped it would.

And now he had to find Annabelle. He had to tell her what he'd uncovered. Something told him that she'd be just as intrigued as he was.

As the last lingering rays of the sun danced over the sea, Grayson took the steps trailing up the side of the cliff two at a time. He knew she'd also want an explanation for his peculiar reaction in the car.

And as much as part of him wanted to avoid her and those uncomfortable questions, there was another part of him that was excited to tell her what he'd figured out. And yet, the conclusions he'd arrived at only prompted more questions. Hopefully Annabelle would have the necessary answers. He just had to find her.

When he reached the patio area overlooking the

beach, he stopped. There before him was a beautiful dinner table set with fine linens and china. It was lit with candles, giving it a warm and romantic atmosphere.

He inwardly groaned, realizing that he'd stumbled into someone's special plans. Someone was going to have a nice evening—a very nice evening. He couldn't even remember the last time he'd wined and dined someone.

Thankfully no one appeared to be about. He made a beeline for the door, hoping to get away without being noticed.

"Mr. Landers," the gravelly male voice called out.

He stopped in his tracks, feeling as though he were back in elementary school. The principal had more than once caught him pulling pranks on his classmates. Sometimes he'd done it just to make them smile, but more times than not it was because he was bored senseless. No one had recognized that he had excelled far beyond his class. Not his teachers and not his parents. As long as he maintained good grades, no adult paid him much attention.

Grayson turned to find out what he'd done this time. "Yes."

The butler stood there. His face was void of emotion. Grayson couldn't help but wonder how many years it'd taken the man to perfect that serious look. Grayson didn't think he could mask his emotions all day, every day. It definitely took skills that he didn't possess.

"Lady Annabelle requested that you wait here for her. She will be here momentarily."

"You mean the table, it's for us?"

The man nodded and then withdrew back behind the palace walls.

Grayson wasn't sure what to make of this scene. He moved to the wall at the edge of the patio. He stared off at the peaceful water while a gentle breeze rushed over his skin. This whole thing felt like a dream, but it wasn't.

He turned back to the table. It was most definitely real. What exactly did Annabelle have in mind for this evening? It was obvious he hadn't scared her off with that meltdown in the car. But how was that possible? Was she used to people freaking out when the paparazzi were in hot pursuit?

"Grayson, there you are," Annabelle crossed the patio to where he stood next to the wall. "Listen, I'm so sorry about earlier. But no worries, I took care of it."

"You took care of it?" He sent her a puzzled look.

"The press. I gave them a statement. I'm sorry that I had to out us."

Out them? His gaze moved from her to the candlelit table with the rosebud and the stemware. What exactly did she want to happen this evening?

He cleared his throat. "You told them about us?" His voice dropped an octave. "What exactly did you tell them?"

Her eyes widened. "Not that."

He breathed a little easier. Sure, the kiss wasn't anything scandalous. Far from it. But he didn't need any more sparks fanning the flames with the media. He had enough rumors following him about and not only did they conjure up horrific memories for him, but they also put his board on edge as it reflected poorly on the leadership of the company.

"Then I don't understand," Grayson said. "Why did you talk to them?"

"So they would leave us alone. I told them we are in negotiations over the South Shore property."

"Oh." That was so much better than anything that had crossed his mind.

"I know that it was presumptive, so I made it clear that no deal has been reached and that we are still in the negotiating stage."

He nodded. "I understand. Did they go away?"

"Actually, they did. They seemed disappointed

that it was all about business. Can you believe that? This is a huge deal for Mirraccino. I thought they'd be excited and asking for an exclusive, but nothing."

Grayson's mouth drew upward at the corners. "I think they were hoping for some romance and the promise of a royal wedding."

She shook her head. "That's not happening. Besides, my cousin just got married a couple of years ago. They don't need another wedding already. I have other things on my mind right now."

"You mean dealing with your father?"

She nodded. "But I don't want to talk about that now. I'm hungry."

He thought of what he'd discovered about the note, but he decided it could wait for a bit. Some food did sound good. He glanced over at the candlelit table and wondered if Annabelle was hungry for food...or was she hoping for more kisses?

Dinner was amazing.

Annabelle hated to see the evening end. This was the most enjoyment she'd had in a long time. Grayson had opened up more about his childhood in Ohio. She wasn't surprised to find out that his IQ was genius level and that he'd grown bored of school. Her heart had gone out to him when she learned that his parents had done nothing to nurture his special gift.

With the dinner dishes cleared, every bit of crème brûlée devoured and the hour growing late, they headed inside. She noticed Grayson had grown quiet. Perhaps he was just tired. They had had a long day. Or perhaps he was still rattled by the paparazzi and the chase back to the palace.

Annabelle had made a point of avoiding the topic during dinner, not wanting to ruin the meal. But perhaps it would be best to clear the air.

"Grayson, about earlier at the university, I'm sorry. I hadn't considered that the press would show up. I know I should have, but I was distracted."

"It's not your fault. I shouldn't have let it bother me."

It did a whole lot more than bother him. "Do you want to talk about it?"

Grayson's gaze didn't quite meet hers. He shook his head.

"I understand." She didn't. Not really. "Have you decided what you'll do about tomorrow?"

This time he did look directly at her with puzzlement reflected in his eyes. "What about tomorrow?"

"You're supposed to leave. But I was hoping after

the visit to the university that I'd convince you to stay and give the South Shore and Mirraccino more consideration. Of course, I hadn't counted on the press messing up everything."

He reached out to her, but his hand stopped midway. He lowered his hand back to his side. "They didn't ruin anything. It was no big deal."

She didn't believe him, but she wasn't going to push the matter. "Does this mean you'll accept my uncle's invitation to stay for the heritage festival?"

A small smile pulled at his lips. "How could I turn down an invitation from a king?"

"He will be pleased." She started to turn for the door to her suite, wishing he were staying for her instead. "You should get some rest."

"Annabelle, wait. I'm staying for more than just that."

She turned back to him, hesitant to get her hopes up. "What reason would that be?"

"Do you have to ask?"

"I do."

"I'm staying because of you."

Though she tried to subdue her response, it was impossible. Her heart fluttered in her chest and a smile pulled at her lips. "You're staying for me?"

He nodded. "I think you did a terrific job today swaying my decision on the viability of establishing my Mediterranean headquarters here. The projections and incentives were impressive and well thought out. And the programs at the university were current and cutting-edge."

"Thank you for the compliment. I hope it all works out." And that he spends a lot more time in Mirraccino. "It's getting late. We should call it a night." Before she did something she might regret—like kiss him again.

"Oh, okay. It's just I had something I wanted to talk to you about."

"Do you mind if it waits? I need to be up early tomorrow. I have a couple of things I need to do for my uncle first thing."

"Um, sure. I'll see you in the morning." For a moment, he didn't move. It seemed as if he was considering whether he should kiss her or just walk away.

Was it wrong that she willed him to kiss her again? Her gaze sought out his lips, his very tempting lips. She'd never been kissed quite like she had by him. It had rocked her world right off its axis. What would one more kiss hurt?

Her heart pounded harder, faster. Her gaze focused on his. Was it her imagination or were their bodies being drawn toward each other? If she were just to sway forward a little, their lips would meet and ecstasy would ensue.

Grayson backed away. "I'll see you in the morning."

Maybe she shouldn't have rushed him off. Maybe she should have said that she'd talk to him as long as he wanted. But he was already walking away. She sighed. Tomorrow was another day. Hopefully it would go smoother than this one.

"Good night."

She turned to her suite. Something told her that sleep was going to be elusive that night.

CHAPTER NINE

HAD HE BEEN imagining things last night?

Grayson assured himself it had been a bunch of wishful thinking on his part. It was the best explanation he could come up with for that tension just before he'd walked away from Annabelle. After all, she was royalty and he was just a techno geek from Ohio. Definitely worlds apart.

Grayson ate his breakfast alone. So far there'd been no sightings of the king or Annabelle. Before coming to breakfast, Grayson had checked her room, but she hadn't been there. She must have urgent things to do. Grayson couldn't even imagine what it must be like having your uncle be the king. The responsibilities must be enormous.

But he had to gain Annabelle's attention long enough to ask her some questions about the cryptic note. And no one he'd spoken to seemed to know where she might be. After breakfast, he checked the gardens and the beach. No sign of her.

He was about to head back upstairs to check

her room again when he passed through the grand entryway. It was then that he noticed a folded newspaper sitting on a table. If he couldn't find Annabelle, perhaps he'd do a little reading about Mirraccino. The more he learned about this Mediterranean paradise, the easier time he'd have selling the idea to his board of directors.

He glanced around for one of the many staff to ask them if he could borrow the paper, but no one was about. He picked up the paper and unfolded it. The breath caught in his throat when he saw a picture of himself.

His gaze frantically scanned the picture. It was of him and Annabelle. They were staring at each other. The photo made it look like they were about to kiss. But that wasn't possible. The only kiss they'd shared had been in the privacy of Annabelle's room. And this photo, it was taken outside, and from the looks of it at the university.

His gaze scanned up to the headline—Hero To The Rescue!

He was not a hero. Why did people keep saying that? He inwardly groaned, his hands clenching and crinkling the newspaper. If he were a hero Abbi wouldn't be dead.

Blood pulsated in his temples. Why couldn't the

paparazzi find someone else to torment? He'd had enough of it back in California after the car accident.

Grayson's attention returned to the brief article. It was pretty much what he'd expected. Innuendos and assumptions. But what he didn't expect was a quote from Annabelle.

"We are together."

She'd said that? To the media? Why would she tell them such a thing? It wasn't true. He'd made sure to keep his distance since their one and only kiss—no matter how tempting he found her. What was she up to?

"Grayson, there you are." Annabelle's voice called out behind him. "I've been looking everywhere for you."

He choked down his outrage at the headline. He could only be thankful that the Mirraccino media hadn't dug into his past, but something told him they would soon. "Apparently you didn't look hard enough." He closed the paper along the fold. "I've been right here."

"I'm sorry things took so long this morning. There was more to do than I anticipated."

He nodded. His mind was still on the newspaper article. "Really? It seemed like you took care of everything last night."

She sent him a strange look as though she didn't know what he was talking about. "I, ah, had some last-minute details to take care of for the heritage festival."

His gaze lowered to the photo of them. It had to have been digitally altered because there was no way he'd looked at Annabelle like…like that—like they were lovers.

"Grayson, what's the matter?"

He wondered if she'd seen the photo yet. "Why do you think something is the matter?"

"Because you've barely said a word to me. And you keep scowling. Now what's the matter? Have I done something to upset you?"

"You might say that." He held out the newspaper. "When were you going to tell me about this?"

She retrieved the newspaper from his hand. Her mouth gaped open. He wanted to believe that this was as much a surprise to her as it was to him, but he couldn't let go of the fact that there was a quote from her.

"Aren't you going to say anything?" His voice came out more agitated than he'd intended.

"You think I did this?" Her free hand smacked off the paper.

"It has you quoted in the article."

"I'm surprised you took time to read it." She

tossed the paper back on the table. "For the record, I didn't imply that you and I are lovers. They did that all on their own. I don't know why you're making such a big deal about this. Surely someone of your position must be used to the media by now."

That was the problem. He was all too used to them. He knew how much their words could cut and he thought at last the rumors had died down. But there hadn't been a word about the accident in the paper. Maybe he was being oversensitive.

He shouldn't have been so quick to think the worst of her. Is that what he'd let happen to him? Had his bad experience jaded him?

"I thought you and I were friends, but obviously I was wrong." Annabelle's voice drew him from his thoughts. "I won't make that mistake again." She turned to walk away.

He couldn't let her walk away. Not like this.

Grayson cleared his throat. "Annabelle, wait."

She hesitated but didn't turn around. Her shoulders were rigid. And if he could see her eyes, he'd bet they were glowing with anger.

"I'm sorry," he said. Those words didn't often cross his lips. But he truly owed her an apology. He couldn't take out what had happened to him in the past on her. "I shouldn't have accused you of anything. I know the media can turn the most innocent of comments around."

She turned to face him. Her expression was stony cold. "I appreciate the apology."

He couldn't tell if she truly meant that or not. He'd really messed things up. He raked his fingers through his hair.

"I've got things to do." Annabelle walked away.

He picked up the paper again and held it before him. He studied the photo of them. Is that really how she looked at him? There was a vulnerability in her gaze as her body leaned toward him. This knowledge started a strange sensation swirling in his chest.

Then his gaze moved to the image of himself. He looked like he was ready to sweep her into his arms and have his way with her. Was that really what he'd felt in that moment? He recalled the desire to taste her sweet kisses once more, but he'd thought he'd covered it up. Obviously, he'd failed. Miserably.

Footsteps sounded in the hallway. He glanced up hoping to find Annabelle returning so that they could smooth things over—so they could resume the easy friendship that they'd developed. But it wasn't her. It was Mr. Drago, one of the king's men.

"Can I help you, sir?" The man was always so formal.

"Uh, no." Grayson returned the paper to the table. "I was just going to look for Annabelle."

"I believe I saw her go out to the patio."

"Thank you." Grayson walked away.

Part of him told him to leave things alone. It was best that they didn't reconnect. After all, it wasn't like he was ready for anything serious. He didn't know if he ever would be. He'd already failed so miserably.

And since that deadly car accident, he'd cut himself off from everything outside his board of directors, and his assistant. He'd forgotten how much he'd enjoyed laughing with someone and just sharing a casual conversation.

Annabelle had given that back to him and he wasn't ready to give it up. He wasn't ready to give her up. Not yet.

What was he supposed to do now? He just couldn't leave things like this. And then he thought of the cryptic note. He hadn't had a chance to tell her his suspicion about it. Maybe that could get them back on friendly terms.

He picked up his pace.

* * *

Insulting.

Insufferable.

Annoying.

Annabelle muttered under her breath as she strode down the hallway with no actual destination in mind. She just needed some space—make that a lot of space—between her and Grayson before she said something she might regret. How dare he accuse her?

Like she would do anything to help the media. What did he take her for? A fool? Or was he just another man who thought she wasn't savvy enough to take care of herself and watch what she said to the press?

Her back teeth ground together as she choked back her exasperation. What was it with the men in her life? She found herself headed for the patio. It was her place of solace, well, actually the beach was. The sea called to her. She stared out at the peaceful waters as the sunshine danced over the gentle swells.

She longed to go for a walk and let the water gently wash over her feet. It was so therapeutic. The more she thought about it, the more tempted she became. After all, she didn't have anything else that needed her attention. Why not go for a walk on the beach?

Without any more debate, she set off down the steps. The warm breeze rushed through her hair, brushing it back over her shoulders. Later, she might go for a dip. It'd been a long time since she'd gone swimming, too long in fact.

She slipped off her shoes and walked to the water's edge. She enjoyed the feel of the sun-warmed sand on her feet and then the coolness of the water as it washed over them.

"Annabelle!" The all-too-familiar voice called out to her.

Grayson.

She groaned inwardly. She wasn't ready to deal with him. Not yet.

She started walking like she hadn't heard him. Maybe he'd get the hint and leave her in peace, but something told her that man hadn't gotten to the position of head of his own multinational company by letting people brush him off.

"Annabelle, wait up!"

He definitely wasn't going to relent. She stopped and turned, pausing for him to catch up. What did he want now?

He jogged up to her. "Mind if I walk with you?"

"Suit yourself."

They walked for a few minutes in silence. Surprisingly it was a comfortable silence. Maybe she'd overreacted too. It just hurt when Grayson thought she'd betrayed his trust. When had he come to mean so much to her?

"I wanted to talk to you about that note you found in your mother's journal. There's just something about it that's not quite right."

That's what he wanted to talk about? A little smile pulled at her lips. "What doesn't seem right to you?"

"It's not any one specific thing. It's more like a bunch of small things. You said the handwriting wasn't your mother's, right?"

Annabelle nodded. "My mother was a perfectionist when it came to penmanship. She would never abide by that mix of upper and lowercases in every word."

"Do you know of your mother keeping secrets? Or sneaking around?"

"My mother? Never." And then the memory of that day at the South Shore came back to her. "Then again, there was that strange man that she was arguing with."

"Maybe your mother was holding the note for someone else. Do you think that's possible?"

Annabelle shrugged. "At this point, I guess most anything is possible."

"Then I'm about to tell you something and I don't want you to freak out."

"Now you're worrying me."

"I just told you to stay calm."

"You can't tell someone not to freak out and expect them to remain calm." She stopped walking. She drew in a deep breath of sea air and blew it out. "Okay. Now tell me."

His gaze met hers. "I think the note is some sort of cipher."

"A cipher?"

"Yeah, a code. A secret message."

"I know what a cipher is. I just don't know what my mother would be doing with such a thing. Surely you must be wrong."

"I don't think I am. Back in college, my buddy and I would write them just to see if we could outsmart each other with some unbreakable code."

"Seriously? That's what you did for fun?"

Grayson shrugged. "Sure. Why not? The party scene just wasn't for me."

"You'd rather exercise your brain."

"Something like that."

"How good were you?"

"Let's just say the government got wind of what

we were up to and wanted to recruit us out of college."

"I take it you didn't accept their offer."

"I didn't. But my buddy did. He works for one of those three-letter agencies."

Wow. She'd never met someone so intelligent that they sat around writing coded messages for fun. Who did that? A genius of course. And Grayson was the cutest nerd she'd ever met.

"So what did this message say?" Annabelle asked, more curious than before, if that were possible.

"I didn't start working on it. I mean, I wanted to, but I wanted to check with you first."

"Yes, decode it. I need to know what it says."

Grayson's brows drew together. "Are you sure? I mean, it could be anything. Something innocent. Or it could be something about your mother that you never wanted to know."

"You mean like she was having an affair?"

He didn't say anything, just nodded.

Annabelle didn't believe it. "I realize there's a lot about my mother I don't know, but there is one thing I do know and that is my parents truly loved each other. She wouldn't have cheated on my father. Whatever is in that note, it's something else. And it just might be what got her killed."

"Have you recalled meeting anyone by the name of Cosmo?"

"I've thought about it a lot and I have nothing."

"You mentioned that you have a brother. Could you check with him?"

She pulled out her cell phone and pulled up her brother's number. Thanks to palace security, they made sure that cell service was available down on the beach.

"What are you doing?" Grayson asked.

"Calling my brother like you asked." The phone was already ringing. She held up a finger for Grayson to give her a minute.

Her brother's familiar voice came over the phone. "Hey sis, now isn't a good time to talk."

"Is that any way to greet your only sibling?"

He sighed. "Sorry. It's just that I'm late to meet Elena."

"Is there something going on with you two?"

"Why do you always insist that something must be going on with me and Elena? Can't we just be friends?"

"When Elena is gorgeous, not to mention an international runway model, no, you can't just be friends. Her days as a tomboy are long gone. Don't tell me you haven't noticed because then I'll have to take you to the eye doctor."

"Sis, enough. We're friends. Nothing more. Besides, you know I don't do serious relationships."

"And that's what Elena wants?"

"I don't know."

"Are you in Paris?"

"Perhaps. Now, why did you call?"

She went on to ask him about the name on the note but made sure not to mention the cryptic message. Her gut told her to hold her cards close to her chest until she knew more.

Her brother didn't recall meeting or hearing of anyone with that name. But it spiked his curiosity and she quickly diverted his attention. He might have his issues with their father, but that didn't mean he wouldn't inform their father of her activities if he thought it was for the best. He was yet another protective male in her life. She was surrounded by them.

As soon as she disconnected the phone, Grayson asked, "So what did he say?"

"He's never heard the name. So does that help or hinder us?"

"It doesn't help us. But it shouldn't hurt us if it truly is a code."

"Oh, good. At last, my family will have some answers."

"Don't go getting your hopes up." Grayson

looked very serious in that moment. "I've been known to be wrong. I haven't started working with it."

Annabelle stopped walking. "Well, what are you waiting for? The note is back the other way."

"You mean you want to work on it now?"

"Maybe my father was right. Maybe there is more to my mother's death than a mugging. Either way, I need to know. I owe my mother that much."

CHAPTER TEN

EVENING HAD SNUCK UP on them.

It was nothing new for Grayson. There were many days that came and went without much notice by him as he pounded away on his keyboard. He couldn't help it. He loved what he did for a living. In fact, he thrived on developing software. Watching a program he'd written from scratch come to life was a total rush.

Running a corporation, well, that was something that didn't exactly excite him. There was a lot more paperwork and decisions that had nothing to do with his computer programs or the functioning of the cafés. And administrative issues seemed to crop up when he was right in the middle of a big breakthrough.

But squirreled away in the palace in this enormous library with just about every edition of the classics on the shelf, he found himself distracted. And it wasn't the moonlight gleaming through the tall windows. Nor was it the priceless artwork on the walls or the artifacts on display. No, it was the beautiful woman sitting next to him.

Annabelle yawned and stretched.

"Getting tired?"

She shook her head. "No. I'm fine."

He didn't believe her. It was getting late and they should call it a night.

"Okay, so it isn't all of the capitalized letters," Annabelle said. "And it's not any of the other combinations we've tried. What else could it be?"

"Let me think." He shoved his fingers through his hair. He'd run the note through a program he had on his computer and searched for different variables. Nothing came up…at least nothing that made the least bit of sense.

She sighed and leaned back in her chair. "Are you sure there's something here?"

"You sound skeptical."

"I am."

"If you want, we can forget I ever said anything."

She didn't respond for a moment, as though she were weighing her options. "It won't hurt to work on it some more."

"There's a message here. I know it. Those random capital letters must mean something."

"I guess I should let you know that I already

signed us up for some of the games at the heritage festival tomorrow—"

"You did what?" Grayson frowned at her. "You probably should have checked with me first. I'm not that sports oriented unless it's on a digital screen."

"Good."

That certainly wasn't the response he was expecting. "Why good?"

"Because then you can't show me up at the games."

He shook his head. "You're something else."

"I hope that's good." She smothered another yawn.

"Let's just say you keep me guessing."

Her eyes lit up. "Good. I never want to be accused of being boring. Now what should we try next?"

"We're obviously spinning our wheels right now. Maybe if we take a break for the night something will come to one of us by morning."

With Annabelle in agreement, they turned off the lights in the library and closed the door behind them. The palace was quiet at this hour. But then again, Grayson had noticed that for the most part the palace was quite tranquil. He didn't know if that was due to the large size and the noise not carrying throughout or if it was a request of the king. It was a lot like living inside a library and every time Grayson went to speak, he felt as though he should whisper.

They stopped outside Annabelle's suite. Grayson really didn't want the night to end. All afternoon and evening, he'd envisioned running his fingers through her long, silky hair. And showering kisses over her lips, cheeks and down her neck.

"What are you thinking about?" Annabelle sent him a smile as though she could read his mind.

He cleared his throat. "I was just thinking some more about the note."

She nodded, but her eyes said she didn't believe him. "Well, you better get some rest. We're going to be very busy tomorrow."

"I'd be better off here, working on deciphering the note."

"And I think you need to get out and experience a bit of Mirraccino. After all, the contract isn't signed yet. I still need to give you a good impression of our nation."

His gaze strayed to her lips before returning to her eyes. "I have a very good impression already."

"Why Grayson, if I didn't know better I'd think you were flirting with me." She sent him a teasing smile. "I must be more tired than I thought. Good night." And with that she went into her room and closed the door.

He stood there for a moment taking stock of what just happened. He'd been soundly turned down. That had never happened to him. In fact, he was normally the one who turned away women.

Annabelle was most certainly different. And it had nothing to do with her noble birthright. It was something deep within her that set her apart from the other women who'd crossed his life.

"I can't believe you talked me into this."

The next morning, Grayson stood in the middle of the road. He hunched over at the starting line of the chariot race. His hands wrapped around the handles of the wooden cart. Why exactly had he agreed to this? And then he recalled Annabelle's sunny smile and the twinkle of merriment in her eyes. That had done in all of his common sense.

And now he was the horse and she was the driver. Go figure. What part of not being athletic didn't Annabelle get? And worst of all, the king was in attendance. Grayson could feel the man's inquisitive gaze following him.

"What did you say?" Annabelle asked. "I can't hear you from back here."

Before he could answer a horn was blown.

"Hold on!" Grayson yelled and then he lifted the front of the wooden chariot and set off.

Annabelle of course got to stand in the rustic chariot. He could hear her back there shouting encouragements. It wasn't helping. Why did people find getting all hot and sweaty so exhilarating? He jogged each morning, but that was for the health benefits, not because he enjoyed it. His favorite part of running was when it was over. He was more than fine with a tall cold drink and his laptop.

Lucky for him Annabelle didn't weigh much. He kept his gaze on the finish line. He'd told Annabelle not to get her hopes up for winning. He was definitely not a sprinter, but now that the race was under way, his competitive streak prodded him onward.

He looked to his right. They'd passed that team, leaving only one other team in this heat. He quickly glanced to the left to find two guys. They were slightly ahead.

"Go, Grayson!" Annabelle cheered. In his mind's eye he could see her smiling. "We can do this!"

She was right, he could catch them. Adrenaline flooded his veins.

He just had to push harder. This wasn't so bad. In fact, he kind of liked it.

"Grayson, straighten up."

He glanced forward and realized that he'd listed to the left. Oops. But it wasn't such an egregious error that it couldn't be fixed. He just had to stay focused. The further they went, the heavier his load became. His leg muscles burned, but he refused to slow down. Annabelle was counting on him.

His breathing came in huffs. He really needed to take his running more seriously in the future. Who knew when the next chariot race would pop up? He'd laugh, but he was too tired.

He was running out of energy. Still, he kept putting one foot in front of the other. The finish line was just a little farther. Keep going. Just a little farther.

He.

Could.

Do.

It.

When his chest struck the ticker tape, a cheer started deep in his chest and rose up through his throat. He lowered the cart. He drew in quick, deep breaths.

The next thing he knew, Annabelle ran up to him. With a great big smile, she flung her arms around him. "We did it! We did it!"

He wasn't so sure how much of a "we" effort it was, considering all she'd had to do was hold on, but he wasn't about to deflate her good mood. He wrapped his arms around her, pulling her close and enjoying the way her soft curves molded to his body.

But then she pulled away—much too soon. She was still smiling as she leaned up on her tiptoes and swayed toward him. She was going to kiss him. That would make this torture he'd gone through totally worth it.

And then something happened that he hadn't expected; her lips landed on his cheek. His cheek? Really? He deserved so much more than that.

Totally deflated, he struggled to keep the smile on his face as the official made his way over to congratulate them and let them know that they would be racing later that afternoon in the final heat.

Yay! Grayson couldn't wait. Not. But when he looked back at Annabelle, who was still grinning ear to ear, his mood lifted. How could he complain when it obviously made her so happy? Besides, it meant that he didn't have to go running later this evening or tomorrow morning. He could deal with that.

When they set off to get drinks, Annabelle glanced his way. "See, that wasn't so bad, was it?"

"If you say so." He refused to tell her that she

was right. If he did, he worried about what she'd come up with next for them to do.

"And I bet you thought all of these old games would be boring. Sometimes you don't need technology to have a good time. Doing things the old-fashioned way can be fun too."

There was something in what she said that struck a chord in his mind. While Annabelle got them some cold water to drink, he thought about what she'd said about not needing technology and doing things the old-fashioned way.

"Here you go." She held the water out to him.

He readily accepted it. He could feel the icy-cold liquid make its way down his parched throat. It tasted so good that he ended up chugging most of it.

"You know, you're right," he said.

"Of course I am." Then she paused and sent him a puzzled look. "About what exactly?"

"Not needing technology. Sometimes old school works."

"I'm not following you."

He lowered his voice, not wanting to be overheard. "The note. I was trying more modern ways of cracking it but I need to try a more old-school method."

"Oh." Her eyes lit up. "That's great." Then the smile slipped from her face.

"What's the matter now?"

"You won the race."

Leave it to Annabelle to confuse him once again. "I thought that was a good thing."

"It was until you figured out what to do with the note. Now we have to stay for the final heat and the note is back at the palace."

"Stop fretting. It isn't going anywhere." He glanced around. "Why don't you show me around the village before lunch?"

She hesitantly agreed and set off. He found it interesting that the streets within the village were blocked off to cars and trucks. The cobblestone paths were for two-legged and four-legged pass-ersby only.

Annabelle pointed out historic buildings with their stone-and-mortar walls. Each building was unique, from their materials to the layout, and even the doors were all different shapes. There were no cookie-cutter replicas anywhere.

Walking through Portolina, Grayson felt as though he'd stepped back in time—at least a couple of centuries. He enjoyed visiting, but he definitely wouldn't want to stay. He had a soft spot for all things technological starting with his computer and microwave.

The villagers were super friendly. Many of them made a point of greeting Annabelle. They didn't treat him as an outsider but rather drew him into the conversation. He'd never visited such a friendly place.

The cobblestone path wound its way through the village, past the tailor, baker and schoolhouse. Whatever you needed, it was within walking distance. It was such a simple way of life. The exact opposite of his high-tech, state-of-the-art existence.

But not all of Mirraccino was locked in the past. This island nation had the best of both worlds. It tempted him to consider purchasing a vacation home here.

He glanced over at Annabelle. She was all the incentive he needed to spend more time here.

He halted his thoughts, startled that he was beginning to feel something for Annabelle. But that couldn't be. He wouldn't allow himself to get emotionally invested.

If he were smart, he'd catch the next plane to Rome. But he'd already obligated himself to decipher the note and there was the pending proposal for the café. He was stuck.

He'd just have to proceed carefully and not risk his scarred heart.

CHAPTER ELEVEN

SHE HAD TO HURRY.

That evening, Annabelle rushed out of the kitchen. She paused in front of an ornate mirror in the hallway to run a hand over her hair. She considered going back to her room to touch up her makeup, but she didn't want to waste any more time. She was already ten minutes late to meet Grayson.

The day had rushed past her in a heartbeat. In between the chariot races, the tour of the village and the quaint shops, they'd sampled many of the local culinary treats. Truth be told, she'd had a fantastic day. She'd had more fun with Grayson than she'd had in a long time. She hadn't realized until then how much she'd let her work take over her life. And that had to stop.

She promised herself that once she finished the South Shore Project she would start living her life and having some fun. If she'd learned anything from her mother, it was that life was too short not to enjoy it. And she enjoyed it a lot more with Grayson in it. He'd been such a good sport that day with the chariot races. And she had a surprise for him tomorrow at the festival.

But now it was time to puzzle over that note again. It wasn't like she could make anything of it. She honestly didn't think there was anything to it. However, she didn't mind spending more time with Grayson while he worked on it.

Annabelle rushed into the library to find Grayson already there. "Sorry I'm late. Things took longer than I'd planned."

He glanced up from where he was sitting on the couch. "No problem. I haven't been here that long. I had a lot of emails to answer and a couple of phone calls to return."

"Sounds like you were busy. I hope there aren't any problems with your business."

"No. Nothing serious. Just the usual things that need answering or approval. If it isn't one thing, then it's something else. I also did some thinking about that note. Do you think Cosmo is some sort of nickname that your mother had?" Grayson asked. "Maybe something from her childhood?"

"Not that I know of. Does this mean you think the note was written to her?"

"It's just a thought."

She stood behind him as he sat on the couch. She leaned over his shoulder, getting a better look at the note. "But if this note was written to her, I'm confused. So she gave someone tea who must have known her when she was a child? It just doesn't make any sense."

"Which is why I think it's a cipher."

She picked up the note and stared at it, wishing something would pop out at her. "In the beginning I thought the chance of this note being some sort of cipher was a bit far-fetched."

"And now?"

"I'm still skeptical but the mix of random upper and lowercase letters is odd. And then there's the strange wording. I mean, do people really say that tea is their gold. Isn't that a bit of overkill?"

"What do you think?"

She moved around the couch and sat down. "Maybe Cosmo is some sort of code name."

Grayson smiled. "Have you been watching a lot of 007 movies?"

She shrugged, not really in a jovial mood. Maybe it was just exhaustion settling in. Or maybe it was her rising frustration. "I just want to know the truth. I want to know if there's more to my mother's death than anyone has acknowledged. Maybe unraveling what exactly happened to her and who killed her will help my father. I don't think he's ever really recovered from the event. He's always worried about me and my brother."

"And you think that if you can figure out what happened then your family can have a normal life?"

"Maybe not normal precisely. I'm not even sure what that is anymore, but something less stressful than what we have now. My father is always worried, checking in every evening. And my brother, well, he says that he's fine, but he's never home. He's always on a new adventure. Last I heard he was in Paris, visiting an old friend of ours. It seems like my family is never in the same place at the same time."

Grayson reached out and took her hand in his. "I'm sorry. I hope you're able to change things. I know what it is to live without any family around. It can get pretty lonely, especially around the holidays."

"Why don't you try talking to your family?"

He shook his head. "That chapter of my life is over."

"A lot of time has passed since you've spoken to them—tempers have cooled, expectations have adjusted and regrets have set in." She didn't want him to pass up a chance to reconnect with his parents.

If she could have one more day with her mother it would mean the world to her. "When was the last time you spoke with them?"

He cleared his throat. "When I got a scholarship to college. I was sixteen."

"Sixteen. Wow. How did you make it on your own?"

"I worked. Hard. I took every job I could find. I ate a lot of ramen noodles and cans of tuna."

"Surely they miss you."

He shook his head. "They made their feelings bluntly obvious."

"A lot of time has passed. Maybe you could try again."

"Annabelle." There was a definite warning tone to his voice.

She understood this was a sensitive subject for him, just as her mother's murder was sensitive for her. If she could pay him back for all of his assistance by helping to find a bridge back to his family, she had to try.

"I'm sure they regret the way things ended."

"Stop." Grayson's body grew visibly stiff. "Now, do you want to go over this note or not?"

Perhaps she shouldn't have pushed the subject of his family so much. "I only meant to help."

"I know." He turned his attention back to the note and then began typing on his computer.

She glanced at the monitor. "Your idea of this being old-school coding, what did you mean?"

"I think this note could simply be a case of letter replacement or taking every other letter or so."

"What can I do to help?"

He explained his plan to unravel the note. It sounded simple enough. She just wondered if it'd work.

Annabelle made a stack of photocopies, even though Grayson offered to write a computer program to sort out the correct letters. She said they could do it just as quickly by hand. And she wanted to be able to contribute. So with copies of the note and highlighters, they started going through the note, highlighting every capital letter without success. Then they tried every other letter, every third letter and so on.

"This isn't working," Annabelle said in exasperation.

"I agree." Grayson studied the note for a bit. "Maybe we're jumping ahead."

"What do you mean?"

He continued staring at the copy of the note. "Perhaps the note is telling us something."

Knock. Knock.

Who could that be? Annabelle sent Grayson a worried look. No one in the palace knew what they were up to and that's the way she wanted it to remain. She quickly turned all of the pages over.

"Come in."

The door opened and Mr. Drago stepped into the room. Annabelle had known him all of her life. He was a quiet man, who never gave any outward signs of what he was thinking. Annabelle had always felt like they were strangers.

"Excuse me, ma'am. The king would like to know if you are done in his office."

"Yes, I am." Did her voice really sound off? Or was she just being a bit paranoid. "Please thank my uncle for me."

"Yes, ma'am. Is there anything I can do for you?"

"Thank you, but I think Grayson and I are good."

"Very well." He looked at her like he wanted to say something else, but then he quietly backed out of the room, closing the door behind him.

Once he was gone, she breathed easier and unclenched her hands. "Do you think he suspects something? Or worse, do you think my uncle is suspicious?"

"Why? Because he asked if you needed anything?"

She nodded. Her mind raced with potential scenarios, none of them good.

"The only reason anyone would be suspicious is because you look like you're ready to jump out of your skin. Relax," Grayson said. "I'm serious. You look like you just stole the crown jewels."

"Not me." She sat down on the couch next to him. "I'd crack under the stress."

"I don't know about that. You seem to be doing fine with our secret investigation."

"But that's different. If this note proves to have something to do with my mother's death, what we're doing is about uncovering the truth about my past—a chance for my family to heal. I'm not out to hurt anyone. Unless you consider the killer being exposed and punished."

"And for any of that to happen, we need to decode this note." Grayson paused and gave her a serious look. "Are you going to be okay if this turns out to have absolutely nothing to do with your mother's death?"

"I honestly have no expectations. Okay, that's not exactly true. I'm starting to believe you. But whether the coded message has something to do with my mother's death is questionable. And we won't know unless we get back to work."

"It's getting late. Maybe we should pick this up in the morning."

"About that...we can't." This time she avoided his gaze.

"And why would that be?"

"Because we have plans."

"Oh, no. Not another chariot race. I refuse. I ache in places that I don't think are supposed to hurt. You'll have to find yourself another horse."

Annabelle failed to suppress a laugh. "I promise it's nothing like that."

"Good. Then what plans would these be?"

"I promise no physical effort will be required, but I'm going to make you wait until tomorrow to find out the details."

"Oh, no. I don't think so." His determined gaze met and held hers. "You have to tell me or else."

She couldn't stop smiling. "Or else what?"

He reached out and started tickling her. His long fingers were gentle, but they seemed to gravitate to all of her ticklish spots. Laughter peeled from her lips as she slid down on the couch. She tried shoving him away, but he was too strong for her.

And then suddenly she realized that he was practically on top of her. He smelled spicy and manly. And her hands were still gripping his shoulders that were rock hard with muscles.

Their gazes met and her heart leapt into her throat. Did he have any idea what he did to her body? Or how much she wanted to pick up kissing him where they'd left off before?

He stopped tickling her, as though he were reading her thoughts. Was it that obvious on her face how much she desired him? And in that moment, she wanted him touching her again, not tickling her, but caressing her. And she wanted his mouth pressed to hers.

Not about to let the moment slip away, she reached up and pulled his head down to hers. She claimed his lips with all the heat and passion that she'd kept locked up inside her. His lips moved over hers with a gentleness that surprised her. His approach was much smoother than her inexperienced clumsiness.

She slowed to his gentle, enticing pace. She found the slow kiss allowed her to enjoy the way he evoked the most delicious sensations within her. She could kiss him all night long. A moan swelled in the back of her throat and grew in intensity.

The note and its meaning slipped to the back of her mind. All that mattered right now was the man hovering over her. She'd never felt like this for a man before...ever. He was sweeter than the finest chocolate cake. And he was more addictive than her caramel coffee lattes.

She had no idea how much time had passed, nor did she care, when a cell phone buzzed. Annabelle knew nothing could be as important as this moment. And apparently Grayson agreed as he continued to kiss her. But the phone kept on buzzing.

Grayson pulled back. The phone stopped ringing. Too little, too late.

He ran a hand over his mouth as though realizing the gravity of what had just happened between them. It wasn't just a passing fancy. There was something serious growing here. Annabelle wasn't anxious to examine it too closely. Everything would be better if they just kept it light and simple.

The phone began to buzz again. Grayson frowned. "I better get this."

Annabelle sat up and straightened her clothes. "Go ahead."

It was funny how things went from very heated to suddenly awkward in a matter of seconds. What in the world had come over her? She remembered their sweet moment of abandon. It had been so good. And so not what they should have been doing together. After all, she still had a deal to sign with Grayson. The last thing she needed to do was complicate matters even more than they were already.

Still… She sighed, recalling the way his lips felt against hers. Heat swirled in her chest and rushed up her neck. She resisted the urge to fan herself.

Annabelle lifted a sheet of paper with a copy of the note. This was what she should be concentrating on, not Grayson and his tantalizing lips.

"Sorry about that," Grayson said, turning back to her. "It was business."

"Um, no problem." She pretended to be concentrating on the note, but she was having a severe problem focusing. "I was just thinking some more about this note."

"Oh, no, you don't." He swiped the paper out of her hand and set it on the coffee table.

"Hey, what did you do that for?"

"Because we weren't finished yet."

Again, heat flooded her cheeks. "Grayson, I don't think—"

"Hey, you owe me an answer and I'm not letting you get out of it."

An answer? He wasn't talking about picking up where they'd left off with the kiss? Oops. She averted her gaze, not wanting him to read her thoughts.

"Well?" he prompted.

She glanced at him, surprised to find merriment twinkling in his eyes. So, he didn't regret what just happened between them, but had she read too much into it? That must be it. She needed to lighten up.

Her thoughts were cut off when Grayson's fingers began tickling her sides again. Why did she have to be so ticklish? How embarrassing.

Laughter filled the air and her thoughts scattered. What was it about this man that made her forget her responsibilities and just want to have fun with him?

Having problems catching her breath between the laughter, she finally gasped, "Okay."

He paused and arched a brow. "Okay, what?"

"Okay, you win." She drew in one deep breath after the other, so relieved that the tickling had subsided. "I'll tell you."

"So out with it. What devious plan do you have in store for me?"

"Eating cake."

His brows drew together. "What?"

"You're a judge for the baking contest tomorrow."

It took a moment for her words to sink in and then a smile lifted his very tempting lips. "I can do that. I like cake."

"There's more than cake. There will be cookies, bread and some other stuff."

He rubbed his flat abdomen. "Sounds good to me."

"I'm glad you approve. So it's a date?"

The startled look on Grayson's face alerted Annabelle to her slip of the tongue. She inwardly groaned. If only it were possible to go back in time, she would. In a heartbeat.

CHAPTER TWELVE

A DATE?

Was she serious?

Grayson's heart was lodged in his throat. Sure they'd had some fun this evening, well, pretty much all day. He hadn't even minded playing the part of her horse for the races. But this was going further than he'd intended.

Granted, he probably shouldn't have given in to his urge to tickle her—to hear her laugh, but hindsight was always twenty-twenty. And then he'd made things worse by kissing her. Or was it that she'd kissed him? It was all a bit jumbled in his mind.

He got up and backed away from Annabelle. Some distance would help them both think clearly. He hoped.

Because there was no way he was dating her—or anyone. He'd sworn off relationships after Abbi had died in that car crash. He couldn't make himself that vulnerable again. He couldn't go through the pain of losing yet another person who he loved.

"I… I'm sorry if you got the wrong idea," he stammered. His heart was pounding so hard now that it was echoing in his ears.

"I didn't." She glanced away and started straightening up the papers. "It was just a slip of the tongue. Honest."

He wanted to believe her, but he recalled the intensity of their kiss. And it sure wasn't just him who had been into it. She'd been a driving force that had kicked up the flames of desire.

Perhaps it was time to straighten a few things out between them. He certainly didn't want her to get the wrong idea and end up getting hurt.

"Annabelle, we need to talk."

"About the note?"

He shook his head. The hopeful look on her face fell and he knew that he was on dangerous ground. One wrong word or look and things would go downhill quickly.

"Listen, Annabelle, I think I gave you the wrong impression." Boy, this was harder than he'd thought it would be. And with her staring right at him, he struggled to find the right words. "I didn't mean to imply with that kiss that there could be anything between us. I… I just got caught up in the moment."

Her gaze narrowed in on him and he prepared himself for her wrath. He was certain that someone as beautiful, fun and engaging as her was not used to being rejected—not that he was rejecting her. He was just letting her know that he wasn't emotionally available. And he didn't know if he ever would be.

Annabelle got to her feet. "I didn't think that this," she waved her hand at the couch, "was a prelude to marriage. I may be a bit sheltered thanks to my father and my uncle, but even I am not naive. Or perhaps that's what you're worried about, my father and uncle forcing you to marry me." Her eyes grew dark and the room grew distinctly chilly. "Trust me. That would not happen. I wouldn't allow it. And I'm sorry you think so little of me."

"That isn't what I meant."

She turned her back to him and began gathering all of the papers. Oh, boy, had he made a mess of things. Where had the smiling and laughing Annabelle gone? And how did he get her back?

He jammed his fingers through his hair. "Annabelle, that isn't what I meant. It's just that, well, I'm not ready for anything serious. And I didn't want you to get the wrong impression. I like you, but that's all it can ever be."

With all of her papers and pens gathered, she straightened. Her guarded gaze met his. "Thank you for sorting it out. I'll make sure that nothing like that ever happens again. And now, I'm going to bed. Alone."

When she started toward the door, he called out, "But what about the note?"

She paused and for a moment he wasn't sure she was going to say anything, but then she turned back to him. "That's not your problem. I appreciate what you've done. But I won't be needing your assistance going forward."

"Annabelle, I'm sorry. I didn't mean to hurt your feelings."

She turned and marched out the door.

Great! Could he have made more of a mess of things?

Frustration balled up in his gut. He felt like throwing something. He'd never felt this sort of overwhelming sense of failure. He'd meant to protect Annabelle and instead he'd done the exact opposite.

Energy built up in his body and he needed to expunge it. But when he glanced around, he knew this was not the place to take out his emotions.

This palace was more exotic than any museum he'd ever visited. He might be rich, but he'd be willing to guess that most of the pieces in this room were priceless. He needed to get out of here.

He headed for the door. There was no way he'd be able to go to sleep anytime soon. He was wide awake and he had a decision to make: cut his losses and leave Mirraccino as soon as possible or stay and try to make this up to Annabelle.

Deciding to burn off some of his pent-up energy, he headed for the beach. The sand was highlighted by moonlight, but he barely noticed the beauty of the evening. His thoughts were solely on Annabelle.

He started walking aimlessly. He had to work all of the frustration out of his system so that he could think clearly. He didn't know how far he'd walked when he finally stopped.

He'd known the truth before he'd even set off on this stroll—he wasn't going anywhere. At least not yet. He had too much to wrap up here, from testifying over the purse snatching to judging at the festival. But he knew those were just excuses. He wanted to stay and make things right with Annabelle. At this point, he had to wonder if that was even possible.

By the time Grayson returned to his suite, his

body was exhausted. After a cool shower, he stretched out on the king-size bed. He closed his eyes, but all he saw was Annabelle's face with that hurt expression that sliced right through him. He tossed and turned, but he couldn't find any solace or drift off to sleep.

He turned on the bedside light and reached for his phone. Annabelle may have taken all of the paper copies of the note with her, but she'd forgotten that he still had a photo of it on his phone. He pulled it up and stared at it for a moment.

For being a genius, he sure hadn't displayed much intelligence when it came to revealing the secrets of this note. What was up with that? He was usually very good at this type of thing. And then the answer came to him. He hadn't wanted to solve the mystery of the note. He liked having an excuse to spend time with Annabelle.

But now that he'd gone and ruined all of that, there was no reason for him not to finish it. Perhaps it could be some sort of peace offering. After all, he wanted Annabelle to find the truth about her mother. He just hoped it would bring her the answers she craved.

He stared at the message. He believed the key to solving it was more obvious than he'd first surmised.

He read it again. *Tea is my Gold.*

Could that mean *T* equaled *G*?

Grayson retrieved his computer and set to work setting up a spreadsheet to imitate a cipher wheel. In the end, he determined that the capital letters and misspellings were red herrings.

He set the cipher wheel with *T* equals *G*. The other sentence in the message referenced the first and forth. After trial and error, he decided that it was referring to the first letter in the first and fourth words.

In the end, he ended up with: *SUNDIAL. FIVE. TWO.*

Grayson went over the message again and again. It always came back to the same thing. He stared at the message. That had to be right.

What were the chances that he'd got it wrong and the words were so clear?

None. This was it.

He was holding the answer that Annabelle had been seeking. But where was this sundial? And what would they find when they got there?

He wanted to go wake her up, but he didn't dare. She'd been so upset with him earlier that perhaps some sleep would improve her mood.

In the meantime, he searched on the internet for a sundial in Mirraccino, but he couldn't find any. That was odd. Was it possible this mysterious sundial was on another island? Or in a different country?

He yawned. At last, he was winding down. He glanced at the time on his laptop. It was well past two in the morning. If he didn't get some sleep, he'd turn into a big grumpy pumpkin come sunup.

Talk about overreacting.

Annabelle made her way to the village for today's baked goods competition. She'd delivered her entry early that morning and returned to the palace to finish some work on another of the South Shore revitalization projects.

The truth was that she hadn't slept much the night before. Once she'd calmed down and gotten over the sting of Grayson's rejection, she'd realized that she could have taken his words better. A lot better.

Did she really have to storm out of the room? Heat rushed to her face. He was honest with her and that's what she'd wanted. She just hadn't expected him to turn away her kisses. Was she that bad at it?

The thought dug at her. Or was there something wrong with him? After all, what did she really know about him? That he lived in California. That he was rich. And that he was estranged from his family. In the grand scheme of things, that wasn't a whole lot of information. Perhaps she'd been saved from an even bigger hurt. She clung to that last thought, hoping it would ease the pain in her chest.

She approached the tent where her triple chocolate cake was to be judged. It was then she realized that she'd forgotten to notify the festival officials that Grayson wouldn't be judging. She was certain after the scene last night that he wouldn't waste any time leaving Mirraccino.

And the fate of the South Shore? Her stomach clenched. She hated the thought of letting down her cousin, the king and the students at the university. Everyone was very enthusiastic about the trendy café.

She would reach out to Grayson after the judging and see if he would still consider taking part in the South Shore. If need be, she'd extricate herself from the project. That would make it simpler for everyone and hopefully give him less reason to take his business elsewhere.

Annabelle stepped into the white-tented area and stopped. Her gaze searched for one of the officials. At last she spotted Mr. Caruso.

She made her way over to him. He'd just finished speaking with someone and turned to her.

"Good morning, Lady Annabelle. The festival is going along splendidly. I was so happy to learn that you're taking part in it this year. As a representative of the royal family, it really helps relations with the citizens."

"And I was very happy to take part. I had a lot of fun." Her thoughts momentarily strayed to Grayson. It wouldn't have been nearly as fun without him.

"I hope you'll be taking part in the community dinner as well as the masquerade ball."

"I'll definitely be here for the dinner. I wouldn't miss it." Without Grayson around, it didn't sound nearly as inviting, but she would not let the people down. "As for the ball, I don't think I'll be able to attend."

"That's a real shame, but we're really pleased to have you here for the rest of it."

She forced a smile that she just didn't feel at the moment. This was the moment when she needed to admit that Grayson would no longer be around and there was no one to blame for that but herself. She'd driven him away.

She laced her fingers together to keep from fidgeting. "There is something I need to tell you. I'm sorry that it's last-minute, but Mr. La—"

"Is right here."

The sound of Grayson's voice made her heart skip a beat. She spun around to find him standing a few feet away. The expression on his face was blank. To say she was surprised by his appearance was an understatement. She thought for sure that he'd already be jetting off for Italy.

Regardless of why he'd stayed, she was happy to see him. Very happy.

But just as quickly, she realized that his presence probably had more to do with the South Shore Project and less to do with whatever was going on between them. That thought dampened her enthusiasm a bit.

Annabelle swallowed hard. "Grayson, what are you doing here?"

His brows drew together. "Did you forget? I'm one of the judges for today's contests."

"Oh. Of course."

Mr. Caruso spoke up. "And we're very happy to have you. Trust me, judging today is definitely a treat." The older man turned back to Annabelle. "What did you start to tell me?"

"Oh, it's nothing. Nothing at all."

She walked away, letting Grayson and Mr. Caruso talk about what was expected of him during today's baking competition. She couldn't deny that she was happy to see him. But what did this mean? Did he regret rejecting her?

And if he did, could she trust him not to hurt her again?

CHAPTER THIRTEEN

"ANNABELLE! ANNABELLE, WAIT UP!"

Grayson had excused himself, telling Mr. Caruso that he'd forgotten to relay a message to Annabelle and that he'd be right back. It wasn't exactly the truth, but it wasn't exactly a lie. He did have something that he had to tell Annabelle, but he hadn't forgotten. He just didn't want to make a scene in front of the man. There was enough gossip going around about them already.

Was she walking unusually fast? Or was he just imagining it? He picked up his pace. He wasn't going to let this awkwardness between them drag on.

"Annabelle." Foot by foot, he was gaining ground on her. When at last he was just behind her, he said, "You can keep going, but just so you know, I'll keep following you."

With an audible sigh, she stopped and turned to him. "Grayson, what are you doing here? I thought we said everything last night."

"Annabelle, I want to apologize."

She shook her head. "Don't. You were honest."

"But there was more I should have said." When her eyes lit up just a little, he knew he had her attention. "I overreacted last night and didn't handle things well. I...I don't know what I was thinking."

"It's for the best." There was a resigned tone to her voice.

"Really?" Surely he hadn't heard her correctly. "You're fine with ending things?"

"Yes. After all, it's not like there was anything serious between us." Her voice was hollow and lacked any emotion. "You made perfect sense."

He made sense? He wasn't sure how to take that.

Her gaze didn't quite meet his. "And don't feel obligated to judge the baking competition. I can make your excuses."

"You aren't getting rid of me that easily." He smiled at her, but she didn't smile back. "I'm looking forward to this."

"I just don't want you to do it out of obligation."

"I'm not—"

"And I hope this won't affect the South Shore deal."

"Business is business. I'm expecting to hear from the board today or tomorrow."

"Good. Now I have to go." She turned and walked away with her head held high and her shoulders rigid.

He blew out a frustrated breath. He'd really messed things up. He stood there watching her retreating form. She'd said all of the right things and yet he didn't believe a word of it.

He might not be in a place for a relationship, but that didn't mean he was okay with hurting Annabelle. He felt awful for his outburst the prior evening. There had to be a way to make it up to her. He wanted to make her smile again. But how?

He thought about the problem for a moment. And then he latched on to the heritage festival. Annabelle had been so excited about it. He thought about the baking contest today. It'd be great if she won, but he didn't know what she'd baked and he wasn't one for cheating. If she won, it had to be on her own merits. That was the only way it would mean anything.

No, there had to be something else. He pondered it some more as he walked over to the tent to get his judging paperwork. He was almost there when the idea hit him. A little payback for Annabelle signing him up for all of these activities. He would now sign her up for an event.

* * *

Second place.

Annabelle shook hands with so many people congratulating her on her accomplishment. She knew that it was foolish and petty, but she'd been hoping to take first place. She wanted to show Grayson what he was passing up by brushing her off.

She gave herself a mental jerk. Since when did she worry so much over what a man thought about her? There had been no one else in her life who had ever affected her so greatly. It was best that he would be leaving soon. She needed to think clearly because she still had a note to decipher. She wasn't giving up…even if Grayson would no longer be helping her.

Having spent a few hours at the festival, and with the baking competition over, it was time she left. She didn't want to have to force a smile on her face any longer. She needed some alone time.

With Berto following close behind, Annabelle was almost to the palace when Grayson came rushing up from behind. His sudden appearance startled her. "Grayson, whatever it is, it'll have to wait."

"Hey, is that how it's going to be from now on?"

She kept walking. "I don't know what you're talking about."

"Yes, you do. You've said all of the right things, but you don't mean any of them."

She stopped and glared at him. "Grayson, what do you want from me? You said there shouldn't be anything between us. I said I was fine with that. And now you're upset because I'm trying to maintain some distance between us. You can't have it both ways."

He frowned as he considered her words. "Would it help if I admitted that I'm confused—that you confuse me?"

"No. It wouldn't." She started walking again. The palace was in sight. Just a little farther.

He reached out, touching her arm. "Annabelle, don't run away."

That stopped her in her tracks. She did not run from anything or anyone. She straightened her shoulders and lifted her chin. She turned to him. "What do you want from me?"

"Nothing."

That was not the response she was expecting. "Then why are you here?"

"It's what I can do for you. I figured out the cipher."

"You did? It really is a cipher?" The longer it'd

taken them to crack the code, the more her doubts had mounted.

He smiled and nodded. "I figured it out last night."

"You did?"

"I couldn't sleep, so I worked on it."

He hadn't been able to sleep last night. The thought skidded through her mind, but she didn't have time to dwell on it. She had to know about the note. "And what did it say?"

"That's the thing. It didn't mean anything to me. I hope it makes sense to you."

"How will I know if you don't tell me?"

"It said, 'Sundial. Five. Two.'"

"That's it?" It sure wasn't much to go on. "Do you think it ties in with my mother's death?"

"The more important question is, do you believe it ties in?"

She gave it some thought. How many people possessed a coded message? And perhaps it would explain her father's inability to let go of the past. But what was her mother doing with a coded message? What was she involved in?

"Annabelle, what are you thinking?"

The concern in Grayson's voice drew her from her thoughts. "I honestly have no idea what to make of this. I've got more questions than answers."

"Then if you're willing, I think we should follow the clue. It will hopefully give you some peace of mind."

"I...I don't know. What if it's something bad? I'm not sure my family can take any more bad news."

"If you want, I can investigate on my own. And if I think it's something you should know, I'll tell you."

Her gaze met his. "You'd really do that for me?"

He nodded. "You are stronger than you give yourself credit for. And you deserve the truth."

He was right. She could do this. She slipped her hand into his. "We'll do this together."

"Good." He squeezed her hand. "Do you know where we can find a sundial?"

She stopped to think. A sundial? Really?

"Annabelle, please tell me you know of one."

Her mind raced. And then it latched on to a memory. "There's one in the garden."

"What garden? Do you mean the palace gardens?"

She nodded. "It's overgrown with ivy now. When I was a kid, my cousins, my brother and some others would play in the gardens. It's a great place for hide-and-seek. Anyway, we stumbled over the sundial."

"Do you remember where it is?"

The gardens were immense. It would take a long time to search them without some direction. But she was certain that with a little time, she could lead them to the sundial.

"Come on." She started off toward the palace at a clip.

It was only when they reached the palace gates that she realized she was holding his hand. She assured herself that it was just a natural instinct and the action had no deeper meaning. After all, he'd made his feelings for her known. Rather, that should be, he had made his *lack of* feelings for her known.

She quickly let go and pretended as though their connection had no effect over her. *Just stay focused on the note and the sundial.*

Annabelle led them straight to the gardens and suddenly it all looked the same. Sure, each geometrically-shaped garden had a different flower. But then she recalled the ivy. That's what she had to search for. They walked all through the gardens. Each path was explored. No turn was left unexplored.

"I don't understand it," Annabelle said. "I know there was ivy here at one point."

"Don't worry about the ivy. Try to remember if

the ivy was near a wall. Or was it out in the open? Was there a statue nearby? I noticed there are quite a few scattered throughout the garden."

She closed her eyes and tried to pull the memory into focus. It had been a lot of years ago and she'd never suspected that she would need to know where to find the sundial.

"Maybe we should ask someone," Grayson said.

Her eyes opened. "No way. We're so close. And I don't need my uncle or father finding out what I'm up to."

"But you're a grown woman. What can they do to stop you?"

She smiled at his naivety. "You obviously have forgotten that my uncle is the king. If he says jump, people ask how high? And my father, he's a duke. He's the one who stuck my security detail on me. There's a lot they can do to make my life miserable. I'd prefer to avoid as much of it as I can."

"Okay. Point taken. But what are we going to do if you can't remember where it is? Or worse, what are we going to do if it has been removed?"

"I highly doubt that it's been removed. If you haven't noticed, my uncle doesn't like change."

"It sounds like you two have a lot in common."

She stopped walking and turned to him. "What's that supposed to mean?"

"It means that you stay here and let them influence your life instead of getting out on your own."

"I left Halencia and my father's home to come here. I can't help that he sent his security with me."

"But you didn't go very far, did you? I mean how much different is your uncle's home from your father's? They both keep a close eye on you."

She didn't like what Grayson was implying. "That's not fair." And worse, his accusation had a ring of truth. "What do you want me to do? Abandon my family like you did?" There was a flinch of pain in his eyes. She hadn't meant to hurt him. "I'm sorry. I shouldn't have said that."

"No. You're right. I did leave my family. Maybe they didn't deserve the way I cut them out of my life. Maybe I should have tried harder."

"And maybe you're right. Maybe I took the easy way out by coming here." Which went back to her thought of visiting the United States. "And once this mystery is unraveled and the South Shore Project is resolved, I just might surprise you and go on my own adventure."

"What sort of adventure are we talking about?"

And then it came to her. "That's it."

"What's it?"

"An adventure. It reminded me that we were

role-playing. The sundial was on the helm of our ship." She started walking.

"And…"

"And it was next to a wall that overlooked the sea." She smiled at him. "Thanks."

"Sure." He looked a bit confused. "Glad I could, uh, help."

They made their way to the far end of the garden where there was a stone wall. They walked along it until they found the sundial.

"It's here!" Annabelle was radiating with happiness.

They both rushed over to the historic sundial. It was made of some sort of metal that was tarnished and weathered. It was propped up on a rock. And just as Annabelle recalled, it overlooked the sea.

"What else did the note say?" Annabelle asked.

"Five. Two."

"What do you think that means?"

"If I have to guess, I'd say five down and two across."

They both looked at the sundial. There was nothing there but the big solid rock and the sundial. Annabelle tried moving the dial, but it was not meant to move.

"Try the rock wall," Grayson suggested, already scanning the area for any sign of disturbance.

Together they worked for the next hour trying each and every stone, but none of them would give way.

Annabelle kicked at the wall. "This is pointless."

"Hey, don't give up so easily."

"Why not? It's obvious that none of these rocks are going to move. There's nothing here."

He had to agree. He didn't think this was the spot. But the note had been so specific. If they could just find the right sundial.

"What makes you think the sundial is here in Mirraccino?" Grayson asked. He couldn't shake the thought that Annabelle and her mother had lived in Halencia and she had found the note in Halencia, yet they were looking here in Mirraccino.

"It's a gut feeling, plus the fact that my mother was murdered here in Mirraccino. It's going to be here." She turned back to the rock wall. "What am I missing?"

"Is it possible there's another sundial around here?"

Just then the butler, Alfred, came up the walk. "Oh, there you are, ma'am." He sent her a puzzled look as she stood in the dirt next to the wall. And then in polished style, he acted as though nothing were amiss. "The king would like to know if you and Mr. Landers will be joining him for dinner."

Annabelle glanced at Grayson. She didn't know where their relationship stood and she had absolutely no idea if Grayson would even be here come dinnertime. And more than anything, she didn't want to stop for dinner. She wanted to keep hunting for the other sundial.

"I had plans to take Lady Annabelle to dinner," Grayson said to her utter surprise. "But if that's a problem, we could go another time."

"No, sir. Not a problem. I will let the king and staff know that you have other plans." The man turned to walk away.

"Alfred, do you have a moment?" Annabelle made her way back to the sidewalk with Grayson right behind her.

The butler turned to her. "Yes, ma'am."

"Grayson and I were just talking about the sundial. Do you know how old it is?"

"No, ma'am, I don't. It could very well be as old as the palace."

"See," Annabelle turned to Grayson, hoping he'd play along. "I told you it was really old."

Grayson's eyes momentarily widened before they went back to normal. "Yes, you did. I just love all of these historical artifacts. Sundials happen to be a favorite of mine."

"Alfred, do you know of any other sundials on the island?"

The butler paused for a moment as though surprised by the question. She hoped he would give them the clue they needed to find the next piece of this puzzle that her mother had left behind for her.

"Actually, ma'am, there is one other. It's in the old park in the city."

"That's wonderful." Annabelle couldn't help but smile. The butler watched her carefully and then just to cover her tracks, she said, "I'll have to show it to Grayson before he leaves the island."

"Anything else, ma'am?"

"No. Thank you."

The butler nodded and then turned and strode off.

"Do you think he suspects anything?" Annabelle asked. Her gaze trailed after one of her uncle's most trusted employees.

"Does it matter? You didn't know about the other sundial, right?" When she shook her head, Grayson added, "Without you asking him about it, we might never have found it."

"You're right." She just couldn't shake this feeling that she'd made a mistake. "Let's go into the city."

"You know, I wasn't lying when I said I wanted to take you to dinner this evening."

"Oh, but I thought you said you didn't want to get involved."

"It's dinner. I want to make it up to you...you know, for the way I acted last night."

"So what does this mean? Have you changed your mind?"

"How about, I want to be your friend?"

Friends? That wasn't so bad. There were even friends with benefits, but that was for another time. Right now, she wanted to find that sundial.

CHAPTER FOURTEEN

FIVE DOWN. TWO ACROSS.

"This is it! This is it!" Annabelle struggled not to shout it to the world. Instead, her excitement came out in excited whispers.

She worked to loosen the stone just as her phone rang for about the tenth time. And again, she ignored it. After dinner in the city at a small Italian restaurant, she'd grabbed Grayson's hand and snuck out the back while Berto waited for them by the front door.

With the darkness of evening having settled over the city, they'd been able to move quickly down the sidewalk. It was only a five minute walk to the oldest park in Bellacitta.

The hard part was searching in the dark for a sundial. Thank goodness cell phones also made good flashlights. And Grayson found the sundial on the north side of the park near a rock wall.

Once again, her phone rang. And just like before, she ignored it.

"Aren't you ever going to answer that?" Grayson asked.

"Not until I'm ready."

"Annabelle, this isn't safe. You shouldn't have ditched your security detail."

The truth of the matter was that she felt bad about slipping away without a word, but knowing Berto's allegiance was to his employer—her father—what else was she to do?

She and Berto were friendly, but he'd never let that get in the way of doing his job. And he was very good at what he did. She'd make sure to protect him from her father's wrath and somehow make this up to him.

"You do know that they're able to trace the cell phone signal?" He glanced around as though expecting an army of royal guards to arrive.

"I know I told you that my father keeps a close eye on me and my activities, but relax a little. I don't think even he'd go to that extent. At least, not yet." She smiled at Grayson, hoping to put him at ease.

He didn't return the friendly gesture. "This isn't safe. What if your father is right and there's a real threat on your life? And your bodyguard, I'm sure he won't be happy about you giving him the slip."

"He never is. And besides, I have you to protect me."

"Wait. You've done this before?"

"Ditch Berto to go treasure hunting? No. Ditch him so I could have some semblance of a normal life? Yes. But not very often—only for really important things." She'd gone through a bit of a rebellious stage as a teenager, but unlike her brother, she'd realized there was more to life than partying. She'd wanted an education and a career. So she'd settled down to study and bring up her grades.

"I don't like this." Grayson glanced into the shadows. "We're going back."

She pressed her hands to her hips. What was it with the men in her life bossing her around? She'd been hoping Grayson would be different. "I'm not leaving here until I do what I intended."

His hard gaze met hers. For a moment, there was a mental tug of war, but she refused to give in. She had a plan and she was going to see it through to the end. She owed her mother that much.

"Okay." Grayson conceded with a frown. "But we have to hurry up."

That was good enough for her. She turned and counted out the rocks, but when she went to remove the stone, it wouldn't budge. The tips of her fingers clenched as tight as possible and she pulled, but it wouldn't move.

"Come help me. This rock is stuck."

Grayson glanced around. "You know if we're not careful, we'll be going before that judge for our own crimes."

"What crime? All I'm doing is moving a stone. And I promise to put it right back."

Grayson sighed but he moved next to her and wiggled the stone out of its spot in the wall. "See. Nothing to it."

She glared at him. "That's because I loosened it for you."

"Uh-huh. Sure."

Any other time, she'd have continued the disagreement, but not today. The important thing was solving this clue. They looked at the stone, but they didn't see anything suspicious about it. It looked like your basic stone. So what now?

Annabelle wasn't about to give up. She moved to the wall and in the dark, she ran her hand around the hole in the wall until her fingers felt something smooth in a groove. The more she ran her fingers over it, the more she realized that it was plastic. She pulled it out.

"It's here!"

"Shh... Do you want us to get caught?"

"Sorry." Annabelle glanced around but there was no one in this part of the park.

Grayson replaced the stone in the wall and joined her on the sidewalk. "Let's go."

"Don't you want to see what it says?"

"It's too dark here. Let's go back to the palace and read it there."

There was no way Annabelle was waiting any longer. Just then her phone buzzed again. She figured she'd better get it before her uncle called out every police officer on the island to search for her. She withdrew her phone. She didn't get a word out before Berto started shouting at her. She could hear the worry in his voice. She apologized profusely and promised it wouldn't happen again.

"So how much trouble are you in?" Grayson asked as she disconnected the call.

"I'm not." When she met the disbelief reflected in Grayson's eyes, she said, "Okay. Maybe just a little."

"And I'm sure your father will hear about it. What will you tell him?"

She grinned at him. "The truth."

"The truth? I didn't think you wanted your father to know about the note."

"Who said I was going to mention that? I was

going to tell them that I wanted some alone time with you."

"Oh. Good idea. That will make him happy," Grayson said sarcastically.

And then without any warning, Grayson leaned down and pressed his lips to hers. At first, Annabelle didn't respond. Where had that come from? She'd thought he didn't want this. Perhaps all day he'd been trying to tell her that he'd changed his mind.

Annabelle had no idea what was up with him but she wasn't going to complain. She enjoyed feeling his lips move over hers. And soon she was kissing him back. Her heart thump-thumped in her chest.

Perhaps he truly did regret what had happened the other night. Maybe it was a lot to compute for both of them. And the evening had been beautiful...in a way. A walk in the royal gardens. Dinner in one of the local restaurants. And now a walk through the park beneath the stars.

Okay, so maybe that hadn't been exactly how the day had unfolded, but who said she couldn't use some creative license and remember the fun parts. And with Grayson's lips pressed to hers, this was the best part of all.

When he pulled back, she looked up at him. "What was that for?"

"So you don't have to lie to anyone. When they ask why you slipped away, you'll have a very good reason." His voice was warm and deep.

She wasn't quite sure what to say. In that moment, she wasn't sure she trusted herself to speak. Her heart was still beating wildly in her chest.

"What?" He studied her for a moment. "You don't have anything to say?"

She swallowed hard. "Yes. Let's look at this note."

Under a light along the sidewalk, they stopped. Annabelle carefully removed the note from the plastic, afraid the paper would disintegrate in her hands, but luckily it didn't.

When she had it unfolded, she asked, "Can you tell what it says?"

Grayson studied the paper. "There's something there, but in this light I can't make it out. We'll have to look at it when we get back to the palace."

And so they set off for home. Annabelle didn't know which had her stomach aquiver—the new message or the very unexpected, very stirring kiss.

This was impossible.

The next morning, Grayson sighed and leaned back on the couch in the palace's library. They both studied the note.

The paper was old and weathered. And worse yet, some of the ink had faded. But Annabelle refused to give up. And he couldn't blame her. If he were in her shoes, he wouldn't give up either.

"What are we going to do?" Annabelle asked, sitting down beside him.

"Find a solution." He opened his laptop and started typing keywords into the search engine about recovering writing from a faded document. Surprisingly, results were immediately available. "At last an answer."

He turned the computer so Annabelle could read the instructions. It certainly seemed easy enough. But would it work for them?

"Let's do it," Annabelle said.

"Are you sure?" he asked.

"Of course. Why not?"

"Because those are some serious chemicals. They could ruin the paper beyond repair."

"And what good is that note the way it is? We can only make out bits and pieces of the message. Certainly not enough to figure out what it says. I say let's do it."

"Okay then. Can you get the chemicals they mention in the article?"

"I think everything should be here at the palace. The trick is knowing who to ask or where to look."

He nodded in understanding. "You find what we need and I'll meet you out on the balcony."

"The balcony?"

"You surely don't want to use those chemicals in here. Do you?"

"You're right." She started for the door.

"Annabelle," when she paused and turned to him, Grayson asked, "you did read the part where the blog post said to let the paper dry for a few hours before trying to read it?"

She frowned but nodded. "This is going to be the longest few hours of my life."

"Hey, no worries. I'll keep you distracted. After all there's the heritage dinner in the village and we have to be at the courthouse soon—"

Knock. Knock.

Annabelle opened the door. The butler stood there holding a big package.

"Ma'am, this was just delivered for you."

"For me? But I'm not expecting anything."

"I assure you, ma'am that it has your name on it. But if you don't want it, I'll take it away."

"Oh, no, I'll take it." She lowered her voice. "I always do enjoy a good surprise."

Grayson couldn't help but wonder why there was only one box. He'd expected at least two boxes. Something was amiss, but he'd straighten it out later.

She moved to the table and set down the big box. The outside cardboard shipping package had already been opened. Grayson guessed that was typical protocol for the palace. He couldn't blame them. In this day and age, one couldn't take chances when they lived in the public eye.

Annabelle lifted out a big white box with a large red ribbon. She glanced at him again. "You know what this is, don't you?"

"I'm just watching."

He enjoyed the childlike excitement written all over her face. Who'd have thought a member of royalty, who could have pretty much anything she wished for, would get so excited over a present. Or maybe the excitement was due to her utter surprise and wonderment. Whatever it was, he wanted to put that look on her face again.

She slid the ribbon from the box. She didn't waste any time and she wasn't exactly gentle. She was certainly anxious to see what was inside. Grayson stood back and smiled.

Annabelle lifted the lid and looked inside. At first, she didn't say anything. His heart stopped. That couldn't possibly be a good sign. The breath caught in his lungs as he waited.

Annabelle lifted the black sequined tulle gown from the box. He'd read the description of each gown on the internet until he found the one he thought would look best on Annabelle. He just hoped he'd guessed correctly about the size. After all, he'd never bought a gown before. But what was the good of being rich, if you didn't splurge once in a while?

She turned to him. Her mouth gaped open, but her eyes said it all.

At last, Grayson could breathe. "You like it?"

She nodded vigorously and smiled. "It's amazing. But I don't understand."

"You will. There should be more in the box."

She turned around and lifted out a Venetian mask with an intricate detail and feathers. "But I...I'm not going to the masquerade ball."

"You are now. It's called payback."

Her puzzled gaze met his. "Payback?"

"Yes, you signed me up for the chariot races and the judging. By the way, I really enjoyed the last part." When a smile lifted her lips, he knew he could get her to agree to go the masquerade ball... with very little persuasion. "And I thought it was time I signed you up for something."

Just then his phone buzzed. He wanted to ignore it, but he couldn't. He was expecting a decision from the board. As he checked the caller ID, he realized it was them.

He moved to the other end of the room to take the call. If it was bad news, he didn't want Annabelle to overhear. He'd need a moment to find the right words. But he sincerely didn't believe that it'd come to that.

A few minutes later, he returned to Annabelle. She sent him a curious look but she didn't pry.

"Aren't you curious?" he asked.

"I figured if you wanted me to know that you'd tell me."

"What would you say if I told you the board unanimously approved the South Shore Project?"

Her eyes widened. "Really?"

"Really."

She cheered and then rushed to him with her arms wide open. She hugged him tight. Her soft curves pressed against him and at that moment, he only had one thought on his mind—kissing her.

He pulled back just far enough to stake a claim on Annabelle's glossy lips. He just couldn't help himself. No other kiss had ever been so sweet. He just couldn't get enough of her.

He lowered his head—

Knock. Knock.

Grayson uttered a curse under his breath as he released Annabelle.

Her fine brows drew together. "Do I even want to know what else you're up to?"

"Me?" he said innocently. "Why are you blaming me for someone knocking on the door? Do you want me to get it?"

"No, I've got it."

She swung the door open and the butler was standing there with another large box. Annabelle immediately took it. A grin played upon her very kissable lips.

"Thank you." She started to close the door.

"Ma'am."

She turned back to Alfred. "Yes."

"The box is for Mr. Landers."

"Oh." Pink tinged her cheeks. "I'll give it to him. Thanks." When the door closed, Annabelle sent him another puzzled look. "What's this?"

He approached her and took the box from her. "This is what I'll be wearing to the ball."

"You're going?" The surprise in her voice rang out, making him smile.

"Of course. I wouldn't make you go alone." When her mouth opened in protest, he held up a finger silencing her. "And before you complain, just remember that you owe me. And be grateful that there'll be no chariots involved and that you won't have to pretend to be a horse." As she broke out in laughter, he'd never heard anything so wonderful. "By my way of thinking, you definitely win."

She subdued her amusement. "When you put it that way, I have to agree with you."

"Good. I'll take that as your acceptance. We'd better get ready to leave for the courthouse."

"I almost forgot." She checked the clock. "We don't have long. I just need to change."

"I think I will too. I'll meet you back down here."

Her gaze moved to the note. "What about this?"

"We don't have time to do anything with it now. Do you have someplace safe to keep it?"

She nodded. "My room will be safe enough." She lowered her voice even though they were the only two in the library and the doors were shut. "As a little girl, I found a loose piece of molding with space behind it. It will be the perfect place."

"Sounds good."

He knew that he shouldn't be so eager to spend time with her. After all he'd gone through after Abbi's death, he'd sworn off letting anyone get that close to him again. But if he could just maintain this friendship with Annabelle, they'd be all right.

CHAPTER FIFTEEN

WHO'D HAVE GUESSED that he could be so charming?

Annabelle's feet barely touched the floor as she made her way back to her room with her ball gown in her arms. She wondered if it'd fit. She wasn't worried. There was a woman on staff at the palace who could work magic with a needle.

She couldn't believe Grayson had bought her a ball gown. No one had ever done anything so thoughtful for her—ever. Annabelle spread the gown out over the bed. It was simply stunning, with a crystal-studded bodice. The man certainly had good taste. A smile pulled at her lips.

If he didn't want to get involved with her, he was certainly sending out the wrong signals, from the kiss in the park to this gown. Maybe he was changing his mind. And she didn't see how that would be so bad.

There was a knock at her door. She rushed over, thinking that it was Grayson. She wondered what he'd forgotten to tell her. She opened it to find a new member of the household staff standing there holding a silver tray.

The young woman smiled. "Ma'am, your mail."

Annabelle accepted it and closed the door. She was about to set the mail aside when she noticed that the top envelope didn't have a postage stamp.

She stared at it a little longer. It had her name typed out but no address. And the longer she stared at it, the more convinced she was that someone had actually used a typewriter. She was intrigued. She didn't know of anyone these days who used a typewriter.

She placed the other two envelopes on the desk before picking up a letter opener and running it smoothly along the fold in the envelope. She withdrew a plain piece of paper. When she unfolded it, she found a typed note:

This is your only warning.
Leave the past alone.
Nothing good will come of you unearthing ghosts.
You don't want to end up like your mother.

Annabelle gasped. She'd been threatened. Adrenaline pumped through her veins. The implications of this note were staggering.

She backed up to the edge of the bed and then sat down. This verified her father's suspicions. He'd been right all along. Suddenly, guilt assailed Annabelle for thinking all these years that her father was paranoid.

Her mother's killer was alive and here in Mirraccino. And this cipher was somehow tied in to it all.

She had to tell Grayson. She rushed out of her room and down the hallway to Grayson's door. Please let him be here. She knocked, rapidly and continuously.

"Okay, okay. I'm coming."

Grayson swung the door open. He was wearing a pair of black jeans and his shirt was unbuttoned. The words caught in the back of Annabelle's throat. He looked good—really good.

"Annabelle, what's the matter?" Grayson's voice shook her out of her stupor.

"I, ah…" She suddenly realized that telling him about the note probably wasn't a good idea. She moved the envelope behind her back.

The more she got to know about Grayson, the more she realized that he was cautious like her father and uncle. He'd probably want to tell the king about the note and she didn't intend to let that happen until she discovered the truth about her mother's death.

"Annabelle?"

"Sorry." Her mind rapidly searched for an answer that wouldn't raise his suspicions. She glanced up and down the hallway, making sure they were alone. Then she lowered her voice. "I just wanted to let you know that I stashed the note." Then she made a point of checking her bracelet watch. "Shouldn't we be going?"

He frowned at her. "I didn't think you'd be anxious to get to the courthouse early."

She shrugged. "It never hurts to make a good impression."

"Annabelle, there's something else. Tell me."

She frowned at him. How could he read her thoughts so easily? The truth was that she really did want to share the contents of the note with him. She'd trusted him this far, surely she could trust him with this too.

"There is one other thing." She glanced around again to make sure they were still alone. She really didn't want anyone to overhear them and report back to the king.

"Would you like to come inside?"

He didn't have to ask her twice. She stepped inside and closed the door behind her. "I received something very strange in today's mail."

"The mail? What is it?"

She held out the envelope. "Here. Maybe it'd be better if you read it yourself."

His brows drew together as he accepted the envelope. He glanced at the front which only had her name, Lady Annabelle. He withdrew the note and started to read.

He didn't say anything as his gaze rose to meet hers. And then he read it again. The continued silence was eating at her. Why didn't he say something?

At last, not able to contain herself, she said, "Well, what do you think? This is a good sign, isn't it?"

"Good? How do you get that?" His voice rumbled with emotion. "This is far from good."

Why wasn't he seeing this as a good sign? Maybe if she explained her reasoning. "Don't you see? If we weren't getting close, whoever this is wouldn't be scared that we're going to reveal the truth."

"And I think you're taking this too lightly. Annabelle, this is a threat to your safety. You have to tell your uncle and the police."

She shook her head. "No way. This is proof that my mother's murder was something more than a mugging."

"Which is another reason to bring in the authorities."

"No." She would not bend on her decision. "They won't take it seriously—"

"They will. They'll make sure you're safe."

"But they won't reopen my mother's case."

"You don't know that for sure."

Her unwavering gaze met his. "We have no proof of foul play. Until we do, this stays between us."

Grayson blew out a deep breath as he raked his fingers through his hair. "You think we'll find the proof we need by following the clues?"

She nodded. "I promise, as soon as we have proof of my mother's murder we'll go to the police."

"Can I trust you?"

She swiped her finger over her heart, making an X. "Cross my heart and hope to die."

"Okay. I don't think you have to go that far. But if I agree to go along with this, you have to do something for me."

"Name it."

"You have to promise not to go out of my sight. Someone has to keep you safe—someone who knows there's a legitimate threat lurking out there."

The implications of his words struck her. "When you say not out of your sight, are we talking about sleeping and showering together?"

He frowned at her. "Any other time I'd welcome

your flirting, but not now. This is serious. You get that, don't you?"

She did, but she refused to let that note scare her off. "I was just trying not to let the threat get to me, but you just went and ruined that."

"You can't pretend your safety isn't at risk." He pressed his hand to his trim waist. "You should back off this search and let me handle it."

"That's not going to happen." She leveled him a long, hard stare, making sure he knew she meant business. "I'll take the threat seriously, but we're in this together."

"And when I tell you to do something to keep you safe, you'll do it without arguing?"

"Now you're pushing your luck." When he looked as though he was about to launch into another argument, she said, "Stop worrying. I won't do anything dangerous. Besides, you'll be right there to protect me. Now, we should get going."

There was no way Grayson was cutting her out of this hunt. They were close to solving her mother's murder. Really close.

"What's wrong?"

Annabelle's voice cut through Grayson's thoughts. They had just finished at the courthouse and had returned to the palace. She'd maneuvered her car into a parking spot off to the side of the palace with the other estate vehicles.

Grayson cleared his throat. "I didn't think you knew how to drive."

It wasn't what he was thinking about, but it gave him time to think of how to word the next thing he had to tell her.

She sent him a puzzled look. "Why would you think that? Doesn't everyone know how to drive?"

He shrugged. "It's just that since I've known you, one of your bodyguards has driven you everywhere."

She shrugged. "I guess it all depends on my mood. But as you noticed, they were right behind us."

"I only noticed because you said something."

"Someday that's all going to change. As soon as we figure this mystery out."

This was his cue to speak up. "I've been thinking."

"I know. You've been quiet ever since the judge gave the kid probation."

That wasn't what had him quiet, but the judge's sentence did give him pause. "Did you think that was a fair sentence?"

She shrugged. "After hearing the kid's side of it,

I can see where desperation might have led him to do something stupid."

The teenager had been trying to help his mother financially. She'd just lost her job and he was scared of how she would make ends meet. It would be a tough position for anyone.

Grayson rubbed his clean-shaven jaw. "I'm just worried the kid might not have learned his lesson. And if he were to be put in a tough spot again, he might make the same poor choices."

"Let's hope not. But doesn't he deserve a chance to prove himself?"

Grayson glanced away. "I suppose."

Annabelle's gaze bored into him. "There's something else that's bothering you and I know what it is."

"You do?"

She whispered. "It's the note, isn't it?"

Needing some air, he got out of the car and she joined him. She kept looking at him, waiting for an answer. He had to find just the right words so she'd give credence to what he was about to say.

He held his hand out to her. "Let's go for a walk."

"But we need to take care of the note and then get ready for the festival dinner—"

"This is important. Come on." He gave a gentle pull on her arm.

For a moment, he thought that she was going to resist, but then she started moving and he fell in step with her. She was headed for the royal gardens, the exact place he had in mind. The gardens were enormous and would allow them plenty of privacy.

With the golden sun of the afternoon shining, it lit up all of the flowers from reds and yellows to purples and pinks. Plenty of greens were interspersed to offset everything. He never considered himself a flower kind of guy, but there was something truly beautiful about this place.

When they came upon a bench along one of the walkways, he stopped. "Let's sit down. We need to talk."

"I'd rather be treating the note so that we can read it."

"That can wait. This can't."

She wasn't listening to him about the threat and he had to find a way to reach her. He needed her to be cautious. But he understood her hesitation to tell her father or uncle. After all, she'd been living with security dogging her steps for years now unless she was on the palace grounds. He couldn't imagine what they might do to protect her if they found out about the note. Before he made the decision of whether to tell anyone about the threat, he had to know that Annabelle was taking it seriously.

"Okay. I'm listening." Annabelle's gaze met his.

"That's the problem. I don't think you're hearing what I'm trying to tell you. This note, it's serious."

"It's proof that we're close to the truth about my mother's murder."

"It's much more than that and you know it." He really didn't want to scare her with the stark possibilities, but what else did he have to knock sense into her?

Annabelle sighed. "I know you're worried. But I can't stop—"

"I know. I know." He understood how important this endeavor was to her.

Annabelle's determination reminded him of Abbi's. That was not a good thing. Warning bells were going off in his head. Maybe if he'd been more insistent with Abbi then they wouldn't have been in that horrible car accident that stole her life far too soon.

He took Annabelle's hand and guided it to his face. He ran her hand down over the faint scar trailing down his jaw. "Do you feel that?"

"It's a scar?"

He nodded. "I'm going to tell you something that I've never told anyone. I mean, it was written up in the papers, but they invariably got the facts wrong. Way wrong."

Annabelle sat quietly as though waiting until he was ready to go on. The horrific and painful memories washed over him. He'd locked them in the back of his mind for so long that it was almost a relief to get them out there—almost.

He cleared his throat, hoping his voice wouldn't betray him. "When my company went public and I ended up with more money than I knew what to do with, I gained instant fame. I could have easily become a partying fool with a girl on each arm, but that just wasn't me."

"Let me guess—you preferred to spend your time working on your computer."

"Something like that. I guess when you grow up with your nose in a book or gaming on your computer, it's tough to change. One night, after a particularly successful deal was signed, a couple of friends talked me into going out to celebrate. Of course, I'm the lone guy at the table while those two were off chatting up some beautiful girls. And that's when Abbi stepped into my life. Literally. I was on my way out when she stepped in front of me."

"And it was love at first sight."

Grayson shrugged, not comfortable talking about

his feelings for Abbi with Annabelle. "She was leaving too. I offered to grab some coffee with her and she agreed. There was an all-night coffee shop a couple of blocks away. I had the feeling that I should know her, but I didn't. And she was actually okay with that. She told me she was an actress. She'd just had her first box office hit. But she wasn't like the others who'd passed through my life. She didn't want anything from me. She was down-to-earth and actually interested in my games."

It'd been a long time since he was able to think about Abbi without seeing the horrific scene of the accident with the blood and her broken body. Those images were the ones that had kept him up many nights. But these memories, he found comfort in them. He remembered Abbi smiling and laughing.

"We became fast friends."

"Uh-huh." The look in Annabelle's eyes said she didn't believe that they were just friends. And there was something else. Was it jealousy?

"Trust me. In the beginning, neither of us were looking for anything serious. We both just needed a friend—someone who treated us like normal people. And so when she wasn't filming or doing promo spots, she came and crashed at my place. We gamed a lot."

Annabelle frowned.

"What's the matter?" Grayson asked.

"I just never had anyone like that in my life. Sure, there's my brother, but other than that my father succeeded in isolating me."

"What about female friends? Didn't you have some close ones?"

She nodded. "I did. But then we grew up and went our separate ways. In fact, my brother is visiting one of our old friends right now. She's a model on the Paris runways. Who'd have guessed, given that she started off as a tomboy contrary to her mother's best intentions? She and my brother were best friends as kids. They'd fish together and go boating. You name it and they probably did it."

"But not you?"

"I guess I was too much of a girly girl. I was not into getting dirty or touching creepy, crawly things." Her face scrunched at the mere thought and he couldn't help but smile.

So once again, she'd been left out. Grayson's heart went out to her. He knew what it was to be alone and never know if the people who were in your life were there because they liked you or because they liked what you could do for them. He couldn't blame her for doing everything she could to solve her mother's murder and to regain her freedom.

When Annabelle spoke again, her voice was soft. "Did you and this Abbi get romantic?"

"Eventually. At the same time, she got nominated for a prestigious award for outstanding supporting actress. Her fame grew exponentially overnight. In the process, she gained what she called a su-perfan. I called him a stalker from the get-go, but she didn't want to believe it."

Annabelle remained quiet.

"Eventually, she told her agent and the studio where she was working on a new film. They hired her a bodyguard until they could do something about the stalker. And everything quieted down. No notes. No roses. No photos. Everyone assumed the guy had given up and moved on." Grayson felt like such a fool for letting himself believe that someone that obsessed would just give up. If only he had done something different.

Grayson leaned forward resting his elbows on his knees. He stared straight ahead, but all he could see were flashbacks of the past. A nightmare that would never fully leave him.

"We felt suffocated and needed some time alone without any security watching Abbi's every move.

So we snuck off to the beach—alone." The breath caught in the back of his throat as he recalled how things had gone from fun to downright deadly. "It…it was like something out of a real-life horror movie." The pain and regret stabbed at him. He lowered his head into his hands. "I keep asking myself, what was I thinking?"

Annabelle didn't say anything. Instead, she placed her hand on his back, letting him know she was there for him. The funny thing was that he was supposed to be here for her—to help her see reason. And yet here she was being supportive to him.

When he found his voice again, he said, "At first, I couldn't even believe what was happening. At a red light on the way to the beach, gunshots rang out from the car beside us. The windows shattered."

Annabelle let out a horrified gasp. "Were you hit?"

He shook his head. "I punched the gas and luckily didn't hit anyone as we cleared the intersection. It turned into a high-speed chase, but I just couldn't shake the guy. And then…"

The scenes unfolded before his eyes. To this day, he still kept thinking "what if?" scenarios. If only he'd made a different decision, Abbi might still be here.

He swallowed hard. "I came upon an intersection with heavy cross traffic. I stopped...the stalker didn't. He...he plowed into the back of my car. It sent us airborne. I can't remember anything other than Abbi's scream. The rest is a blank. The first responders said that I was thrown free, but Abbi, she, uh, was pinned under the wreckage."

"I'm so sorry." While her one arm was still draped over his back, her other hand gripped his arm. "You don't have to go into this—"

"Yes, I do. You have to understand."

"Understand what?"

He had to keep going. He had to make Annabelle understand that risky decisions had major consequences. "Abbi died on the way to the hospital. And it was my fault."

"No, it wasn't." Annabelle's voice was soft and gentle like a balm on his scarred heart.

Grayson turned to face her. "I wish I could believe that. I really do. But it was my idea to go to the beach. It...it was my idea for us to spend some time alone. I just never thought that guy was still sticking around. I failed her."

Annabelle pulled him close and held him. He knew he didn't deserve her sympathy when he was sitting here while Abbi was gone. Life wasn't fair. That's one thing his father had taught him that had been right.

When he gathered himself, he pulled back. "The media, they got ahold of the story, and they told lie upon lie about me and about Abbi. It got so bad that I didn't leave my house for a long time. I worked remotely. That's when I started working on my plan to take the cafés global."

"I'm very sorry that all of that happened to you, but why did you tell me?"

"Because I need you to take that note seriously. Abbi and I didn't take her threat seriously enough and look what happened."

Her gaze met his. "You are that worried about me?"

"Yes. I couldn't stand for anything to happen to you."

"It won't."

"Promise me that you'll be careful."

"I promise."

And then he claimed her lips, needing to feel her closeness. Her touch was rejuvenating and eased away the painful memories. He'd never forget what happened, but he knew now that he had to keep going forward because his life's journey wasn't complete. Maybe he was meant to be here and keep Annabelle safe.

But as her lips moved beneath his, something very profound struck him. Here he was warning her about unknown dangers and yet, he was the one in imminent danger—of losing his heart, if he wasn't careful.

CHAPTER SIXTEEN

"THIS IS A MOMENT we've been waiting for." The king's deep voice rang out loud and clear.

Annabelle quietly sat at the heritage dinner that evening. Back at the palace the note had been brushed with chemicals that hopefully would illuminate the print on it. And while she waited, she'd been treated to the most amazing home-cooked food.

She wasn't alone in her enjoyment. Everyone had oohed and aahed over the entrees before devouring them. And the sinfully delightful desserts had just been served, but before people could dive in, the king wanted to make a special toast.

Grayson sat next to her at the long wooden table. They were having dinner in the village streets of Portolina. It was a community affair and this was the only spot big enough for such a large turnout. Annabelle smiled as she gazed around at so many familiar faces.

Her eyes paused on the man next to her—Grayson. He'd surprised her today when he'd opened up to her with what must have been one of the most tragic moments of his life. And the fact that he'd done it because he was worried about her was not lost on her. This man who said that he wasn't interested in a relationship was now throwing out very confusing signals.

And the fact that he'd been willing to keep her secret for just a little while longer made him even more attractive. He was not like the other men in her life. He was not domineering and insistent on having his way. He was willing to listen and consider both sides of the argument. That was a huge change for her. And it was most definitely a big plus in her book.

Not to mention she was getting used to having him next to her—really used to it. She didn't know what she was going to do when he left Mirraccino. Because no matter what was growing between them, she realized that he intended to leave and return to his life in California.

"And that's why I'd like you to help me welcome Mr. Grayson Landers," the king's voice interrupted Annabelle's thoughts.

Applause filled the air as Grayson got to his feet. He smiled and winked at Annabelle before he made his way toward the king. Hands were shaken. The contract for the South Shore Project was signed. And Grayson offered a brief thank-you.

Annabelle hadn't realized how much this moment would mean to her. She thought that it would be monumental because at last she could show her father that she could take care of herself. But she realized that this moment meant so much more because Grayson now had a permanent tie to Mirraccino. He would be housing his Mediterranean operations right here in addition to starting one of his famous cafés. Maybe it wasn't such a far-fetched idea to think that they might have the beginning of something real.

"Annabelle."

She turned to find her father standing behind her. "Poppa, what are you doing here?"

"Is that the way you greet your father?"

"Sorry." She moved forward to give him a kiss on the cheek followed by a hug. "I didn't know you were coming."

"We need to talk." His voice was serious, as was the expression on his face.

She started to lead him away from the crowd. "Is something wrong?"

"Yes, it is."

Fear stabbed at her heart. It had to be serious

for him to come all of this way on the spur of the moment. And then a worst-case scenario came to mind. "Is it Luca? Has something happened to him?"

"No."

She let out a pent-up breath. She could deal with anything else. Curiosity was gnawing at her. "What is it?"

"We'll talk about it back at the palace."

Annabelle walked silently next to her father. He was never this quiet unless he was really agitated. She had a sinking feeling that she knew the reason for his impromptu visit. And this evening was most definitely not going to end on a good note.

Annabelle stopped walking. "Let's have it out here."

Her father sighed as he turned to her. "Don't be ridiculous. We're not going to talk out here in public."

"There's no one within earshot. And I don't need the palace staff overhearing this and gossiping." She wasn't about to say that there was someone out there who thought they had a vested interest in anything having to do with her mother's murder. Right now, she wasn't sure who she could trust and who she couldn't.

"Fine." Her father crossed his arms and frowned

at her just as he had done when she was a little girl and had gotten into the cookies right before dinner. If only this problem were so easy to remedy. "I know what you did. I know you stole some of your mother's belongings."

"Stole? Really?" The harsh word pierced her heart, but she refused to give in to the tears that burned the backs of her eyes. "She was my mother—"

"And her journal is none of your business."

"I disagree. I was robbed of really getting to know her. And you…you shut down any time I ask about her. How else am I supposed to get to know her?"

Her father's eyes widened with surprise. "Why can't you just leave the past alone?"

"How am I supposed to do that when you can't let go of it?"

Her father's gaze narrowed in on her. "There's more going on here, isn't there?"

"No." She realized that she'd said it too quickly. She'd never been capable of subterfuge and her brother never let her forget it.

"Whatever you're up to, daughter, I want it stopped. Now!" Her father so rarely raised his voice that when he did, he meant business.

"Is there a problem here?" Grayson's voice came from behind her.

She'd been so caught up in her heated conversation with her father that she hadn't even heard Grayson's footsteps on the gravel of the roadway. But she should have known that he wouldn't be far behind. He'd said he'd be keeping a close eye on her.

Her father didn't make any motion to acknowledge Grayson. Instead he continued to stare at her, bullying her into doing as he commanded. And as much as she loved him, she just couldn't abide by his wishes anymore. Their family was falling apart under the strain of what had happened to their mother. She could no longer bear the mystery, the silence, the not knowing. Someone had to do something and it looked like it was going to be her.

"Poppa, I'd like you to meet Mr. Grayson Landers. He has just bought the last property in the South Shore piazza."

The two men shook hands. All the while her father eyed up Grayson. She wasn't sure what was going through her father's mind, but she'd hazard a guess that it wasn't good.

Now was her chance to make her move. "Poppa, now that I've concluded the South Shore Project on my own, surely you must recognize that was quite an accomplishment."

Her father's bushy eyebrows rose. "Yes, you're right. You did a very good job. I'm sorry I didn't say something sooner. As you know, I had other matters on my mind."

"I understand." So far, so good. "Now you have to accept that I can take care of myself. I'd like the security removed."

"No." There was a finality in his voice.

She'd heard that tone before and knew that arguing was pointless. When her father made up his mind, he didn't change it—even when he was wrong. "One of these days you'll have to let go of me."

Her father turned to Grayson. "I see the way you look at my daughter and the way she looks at you. Make sure you take care of her."

Without hesitation, Grayson said, "I will, sir. I promise."

And then her father turned toward the palace, leaving them in the shadows as the sun set. Annabelle let out a sigh.

Grayson cleared his throat. "So that was your father?"

"The duke himself. I take it he wasn't what you were expecting."

"I guess I was just hoping that he would be warmer and friendlier than you'd portrayed."

"He used to be…when my mother was alive. Her death changed us all."

"I'm sorry." And then Grayson drew her into his strong arms. She should probably resist, but right now the thought of being wrapped in his embrace was far too tempting.

The best thing she could do was give her father time to disappear to the study for his evening bourbon and then she would head inside. She was anxious to see if they could read the note yet.

Nothing was ever easy.

Grayson sighed. The initial treatment with the note hadn't worked. Some more research on the internet had them searching for yet another chemical. But it was harder to locate and required a trip into the city. Annabelle had insisted on driving. She'd said it calmed her down when she was worked up. And so with her security in the vehicle behind them, they made yet another jaunt into the city.

This trip had been short and to the point. There had been no time for a walk around the South Shore or a stroll through the picturesque university campus. There hadn't even been a few minutes for some ice cream on this warm day. No, today they both wanted to solve this latest clue.

Like the duke, Grayson was worried about Annabelle's safety. If he could solve this mystery on his own, he would. But he didn't know the island well enough in order to make sense of the clues— for that he needed Annabelle.

This application just had to work. Annabelle and her family deserved some answers. It wouldn't bring back Annabelle's mother, but it might give them all a little peace.

"Well, come on," she said before she alighted from the car.

Grayson opened the car door and with the necessary supplies in hand, he called out, "Hey, wait for me."

She did and then they headed inside. Annabelle agreed to retrieve the note from her hiding spot and meet him in his room. He had a feeling that the weathered paper wouldn't hold up much longer so they had to get it right this time.

When the lock on his door snicked shut, he noticed how Annabelle fidgeted with the hem of her top. Was she nervous about being alone with him? Was she secretly hoping more would happen than revealing the contents of the note?

Maybe a little diversion would help them both

relax. His gaze moved to Annabelle's full, glossy lips. He took a step closer to her. What would it hurt to indulge their desires?

"Don't even think about it." And then a little softer, she said, "We don't have time."

Not exactly a rejection—more like a delay of the game. He smiled. He could work with that.

His gaze met hers. "There's always time."

She crossed her arms and arched a brow, letting him know that she meant business.

He sighed, thinking of the delicious moment they'd missed out on. But then he recalled the ball that evening and his mood buoyed. Soft music, Annabelle in his arms and the twinkling stars overhead. Oh, yeah. This was going to be a great night.

"You're right." He moved to the desk near the window. "Let's get to work."

While Annabelle peered over his shoulder, he applied the solution. All the while, he willed it to work.

At first, there was nothing and then there were the faintest letters. Together they worked, making out the wording of the note. Thankfully the person had used the same key, making decoding it quite simple.

"We did it!" Annabelle beamed.

"Yes, but what does 'Placard. Two. Three.' mean?"

The smile slipped from her face. "I have no idea."

He studied the note making sure he hadn't made a mistake. "What do you think we'll find this time?"

When Annabelle didn't respond, Grayson glanced up at her. Lines had formed between her brows and her lips were drawn down into a frown. Oh, no. There was a problem.

"Annabelle?" She didn't respond as though lost in her thoughts. He cleared his throat and said a little louder, "Annabelle, did you remember something? Do you know what this note is referencing?"

This time her gaze met his and she shook her head. "I haven't a clue."

"But something's bothering you."

She glanced away. "It's just the not knowing. It's starting to get to me."

Was that it? Or was she having second thoughts about unearthing the past? He needed to give her an out. "If you've changed your mind, we can put the note away and forget that we found it—"

"No. I can't. My mother deserves better than that."

But it wasn't her mother he was worried about right now. "You have time to think about it. We can do whatever you want." He consulted his wristwatch. "And now it's time to get ready for the ball."

"I'm not going." She stated it as though it were nonnegotiable.

She might be stubborn, but he was even more so. "You have to." When her gaze met his, he said, "You're my date. And I've never been to a masquerade ball. Look," he walked over to the bed and picked up his black mask, "I'm all set to be your mystery man."

That elicited a slight smile from her, but she was quiet. Too quiet.

"And you can be my seductive lady of intrigue," he said, trying to get her to loosen up so she could enjoy the evening."

"Intrigue, huh?"

He nodded, anxious to see her in the gown. He'd never bought clothes for a woman before. And now he wanted to see if his hard work had paid off. "You'd better hurry. You don't want to be late for the ball."

"But what about the note?"

He frowned. Maybe she needed a dose of reality. "You know how you accused your father of being all caught up in the past?" When she nodded, he added, "Well, you're getting just as caught up in this note. It's not healthy."

Her gaze narrowed. "You don't understand—"

"I do understand. Just remember who has stood

by you through all of this. I want you to know the truth, but I also want you to realize that there's more to life than that note, than the past. Tonight we go to the ball. And tomorrow we will work on solving the message. Agreed?"

She didn't say anything.

"Annabelle?"

"Fine. Agreed."

Knock. Knock.

When Annabelle opened the door, Mrs. Chambers stood there. Her silver hair was twisted and pinned up. Her expression was vacant, not allowing anyone to see her thoughts about finding Annabelle in Grayson's room. Not that he cared what anyone thought.

The woman said, "Ma'am, I came to help you dress for the ball."

"I'll be right there."

"Yes, Ma'am. I'll wait for you in your room." The woman turned and walked away.

Annabelle waited a moment before she said, "Do you think she overheard us talking about the note?"

He had absolutely no idea, but he knew that Annabelle was already stressed. "I don't think we were loud enough for her to hear us through the door." He moved to her side and brushed his fingers over her cheek. "Just give me tonight and I'll give you my undivided attention tomorrow."

She stepped closer. "Does that mean no laptop?"

He readily nodded, which was quite odd for him. Normally he felt most at ease when his fingers were flying over the keyboard typing code or answering emails. His hands wrapped around Annabelle's waist. But tonight, his hands felt much better right here.

"No laptop." He leaned forward and pressed a quick kiss to her lips.

When he pulled back, her eyes were still closed. They fluttered open. The confusion about why he'd pulled away so quickly was reflected in them.

"There will be more of that later." He had no doubts. "But first you need to change. It wouldn't do for Cinderella to be late to the ball."

"When you put it that way, you have a deal." She lifted up on her tiptoes and pressed a kiss to his lips.

Before he could pull her close again, she stepped out of his reach. A naughty smile lit up her face. "We have a ball to attend."

He sighed. Suddenly the ball didn't sound like that great an idea, but Annabelle was already out the door. He shook his head. This evening was going to be far more complicated than he ever imagined. Because there was more to those kisses than either of them was willing to admit.

And yet this evening was going to be a once-in-a-lifetime experience. A ball attended by a king and a duke. And Grayson would have the most beautiful woman in his arms...all night long.

The answer could wait.

Now that the moment of truth was almost here, Annabelle wasn't so sure she was doing the right thing. What if she learned something bad about her mother?

Annabelle's stomach quivered with nerves. What exactly had her mother gotten herself mixed up in? Did her father secretly know? What if all this time he'd been trying to protect her mother's memory? The thought sent a chill down Annabelle's spine.

She scanned the party guests for her father. At last, she found him talking with one of the village elders. He had come alone to the ball and she knew that he would leave alone too. She did not want to end up like him.

Now wasn't the best time to speak to her father, but she couldn't stand the tug of war going on within herself. She had to know.

She made her way over to him. "Good evening, Poppa."

"Hello, daughter. Shouldn't you be with your date?"

Her stomach churned. She was in no mood to make polite chitchat. The best way to end her agony was just to get it out there. "Do you know why Momma was murdered?"

Instantly the color drained from her father's face. "Annabelle, what's the meaning of this?"

"You said you didn't think she died as a result of a mugging, but do you know what did happen?" And then a thought popped into her mind and she uttered it before her brain could process the implications. "Are you afraid that she did something wrong and it got her killed?"

The color came rushing back to her father's face. His voice came out in hushed tones but there was no mistaking the fury behind each word. "Annabelle, I will not stand for you speaking to me like this. I've done nothing to warrant such hostility and suspicion."

He was right. She'd let her imagination get the best of her. "I'm sorry, Poppa. It's the not knowing. I can't take it anymore."

"Do you honestly think your mother would have done anything to hurt our family? She loved us with every fiber of her being." His eyes glistened with unshed tears. "I miss her so much."

"I miss her too."

"She would have been proud of the young woman you've grown into."

"Thank you."

"For what?"

"Talking about Momma. You never want to talk of her and it hurts because I miss her too. And talking about her keeps those memories alive for me."

Her father cleared his throat. "I'm sorry I failed you in that regard. I will try to do better."

"And I'm sorry my questions hurt you."

They hugged and Annabelle accepted that was the best she could hope for from her father tonight. She decided to go in search of her dashing escort. She didn't care how many balls she attended, they were all magical. But this evening was extra special thanks to Grayson.

Tonight, she would laugh, forget about her problems and kick up her heels. Grayson would make sure of it. And tomorrow, her feet would land back in reality. But tomorrow was a long way off.

Her gaze sought out Grayson, who looked so handsome in his black tux. She was in absolutely no hurry for the sun to rise on a new day because she had a gut feeling that tomorrow would bring her those long-sought-after answers. And she had absolutely no idea if those answers would be good or bad.

"Here you go." Grayson stepped up to her and held out a glass of bubbly. When she accepted it, he held up his glass to make a toast. "Here's to the most beautiful woman at the ball."

Heat rushed to her cheeks as she smiled. The truth of the matter was that she felt a bit overdone. The king had sent along a tiara for her to wear. As far as tiaras went, at least it wasn't big and showy, but it just felt like too much.

"Thank you for the kind words."

"They aren't just words. I mean them." He leaned forward and planted a quick kiss on her lips.

He pulled back before she was ready for him to go. A dreamy sigh passed her lips. If only…

Thoughts of her gown and tiara slipped to the back of her mind. Her heart tap-danced in her chest as Grayson smiled at her. How had she gotten so lucky?

The evening took on a life of its own. She sipped at the bubbly. She talked with the guests. And then Grayson held out his hand to escort her onto the dance floor.

In his very capable arms, she glided around like she was on a cloud. She wasn't even sure if her feet ever touched the ground. And her cheeks grew sore from all of the smiling. But she couldn't stop. This was the most amazing evening and she didn't want it to end...not ever.

Grayson stopped moving.

Annabelle sent him a worried look. "What's the matter?"

"Look up."

She tilted her chin upward. "I don't see anything but darkness."

"And..."

"And a star." She smiled. "Are you making a wish upon that star?"

"Perhaps."

Well, he wasn't going to be the only one to make a wish. She closed her eyes and Grayson's image filled her mind. There was something about him that she couldn't resist. She wished...she wished...

And then his lips pressed to hers. Oh, yes, that's what she wished.

CHAPTER SEVENTEEN

THE FAIRYTALE WAS winding to a close.

The ball was over, but Annabelle was not ready to lose all of her glittery goodness and turn back into a pumpkin. With Grayson by her side, the magic would continue long after the last song finished and the twinkle lights dimmed.

"What are you smiling about?" Grayson's voice broke into her thoughts as they paused outside her bedroom.

"Nothing." Annabelle continued to smile as she had all evening. She couldn't help it. She couldn't remember the last time she was this happy. And she didn't have any intention of letting this evening end.

Grayson's mouth lifted ever so slightly at the corners. "Oh, you have something on your mind."

"How do you know? Do you read minds now?"

"No. But your eyes give you away."

He was right. She did have something on her mind. And as delicious as the thought was, she wasn't sure she should follow her desires. But then again, what was holding her back now?

The deal for the South Shore had been signed. If she didn't act now, it'd be too late. Grayson would be leaving for California and she'd be left with nothing but regrets.

Her heart pounded in her chest. Tonight the moonlight and the sweet bubbly had cast a spell over her. She was falling for Grayson in a great big way.

But if she were honest with herself, this thing—these feelings—had started when he'd played her hero and saved her mother's journal from the would-be thief. There had been something special about Grayson from the very start.

And now she was ready to take the next step—one that she didn't take lightly. She'd never outright asked a man to spend the night. She wasn't even sure what to say. But tonight she was feeling a little bit naughty, uncharacteristically bold, and a whole lot reckless.

She opened the door.

"Well, I'll see you in the morning." Grayson turned to walk away.

Oh, no. She wasn't letting him get away. She needed to do something quick, but what? "Grayson, wait."

He turned back. "What is it?"

"I need your help." Without any further explanation, she took his hand to lead him into the bedroom.

But he didn't move. "Annabelle, I don't think this is a good idea."

She turned to him, not about to let logic rain on their magical night. "Why Grayson, what do you think I'm going to do?" Her voice lowered to a sultry level. "Take advantage of you?"

He didn't say anything at first. "The thought had crossed my mind."

"Tsk. Tsk." She gave his hand another pull. "Come on. I promise to keep my hands to myself...unless you'd rather I didn't. And besides, you did agree to stay with me until we solve the mystery of the note."

Grayson groaned. And she grinned like a Cheshire cat. Without a word, he followed her into the darkened room. Something told her that his capitulation was out of pure curiosity and the fact that no matter how much he wanted to deny this thing between them, he simply could not.

"You might want to close the door," she suggested without making any effort whatsoever to turn on the light.

"Annabelle—"

"Trust me." She moved toward the bed.

He groaned again and inwardly she laughed. Who knew Grayson could be so much fun? Or maybe the fun was in her being bold and sassy. Her smile broadened.

When the door snicked shut, she could hear Grayson's soft footsteps behind her. He wanted this night as much as she did. He hadn't been with anyone since his girlfriend, which was understandable and even a bit admirable, but it was time he moved on. It was time that she spread her wings with a man who wasn't intimidated by her father or her security team. And a man who took her opinions seriously.

"Can you unzip me?" She wished she could see the look on his face right now.

"I… I shouldn't be doing this."

"If you don't, I'll have to sleep in this beautiful gown," she said as innocently as she could muster. "Mrs. Chambers already went to bed. She never goes to the ball. And I can't reach the zipper."

He stepped closer. In the next moment, his fingers were touching the bare skin of her upper back, sending shivers of excitement tingling down her spine. He sucked in an unsteady breath. Millimeter by millimeter the zipper came undone. His fingertips were surprisingly smooth. His touch was being tattooed upon her mind.

This was the sweetest torture she'd ever experienced. And then her gown floated to the ground, landing in a fluffy heap. With nothing but moonlight streaming in through the tall windows to see by, she stood there in her black bustier and organza petticoat.

She didn't move. She could feel his gaze on her. The breath caught in her lungs. What was he thinking? Did he want her as much as she wanted him?

Desire and anticipation mounted within her. This was the most exquisite moment as they stood at the fork in their relationship. No matter which direction they took, after tonight, things would never be the same again.

And then his hands gently caressed her shoulders. His touch was arousing. She imagined turning in his arms and pressing her lips to his mouth, but she didn't. Not yet. She knew what she wanted, but she wasn't sure if he'd overcome the ghosts from his past. For this to work, for this to be right, he had to be all-in too.

His thumbs moved rhythmically over her skin. "Annabelle, are you sure?"

She blew out the pent-up breath. "I am. Are you?"

His response came in the form of a gentle kiss

on her neck. She inhaled swiftly, not expecting such a telling response. Not that she disapproved. Quite the opposite. Most definitely the opposite.

CHAPTER EIGHTEEN

"How long have you been up?"

Grayson's deep, gravelly voice came from the doorway of the library. Annabelle was wide awake, showered and working to find the answer to the clue in the latest note. She glanced up from one of the history books of Mirraccino.

When she saw Grayson, memories of being held in his arms came rushing back to her. Along with the memories came the emotions—powerful emotions that sent her heart racing. Last night had been so much more than she'd ever envisioned.

She was in love with Grayson.

And she had never been so scared.

She'd never been in love before. She'd never wanted to let another man into her life. She already had enough men telling her what to do, why add one more? But Grayson was different. He spoke his opinion, but left room for her response.

The truth of the matter was that she could imagine keeping him around, but never once last night or any time since she'd known him had he mentioned sticking around or inviting her to be a part of his life. He'd warned her in the beginning that he wasn't in this for anything serious. She remembered that moment quite vividly. Why hadn't she listened to him then? Now she'd complicated everything exponentially.

"Annabelle, what's wrong?" Grayson approached her, concern written all over his face.

She held up her hand, maintaining an adequate distance between them. She couldn't bear for him to touch her. And she refused to give in to the tears that were stinging the backs of her eyes. This was her problem to deal with, not his. He hadn't done anything but what she'd asked him to do.

"I... I'm fine."

"You don't look fine. Listen, if this is about last night—"

"It's not. And I'd prefer not talking about it." She couldn't stand the thought of him letting her down gently. She could just imagine him giving her some sort of pep talk.

Grayson raked his fingers through his hair. "I knew that last night was a mistake. I didn't mean to—"

"Stop." Then realizing she'd raised her voice while the door to the hallway was standing wide open, she lowered her voice. "It wasn't a mistake. You have nothing to feel bad about." And she just couldn't talk about it any longer. "And I have to go out. If you need anything just ask the staff."

She started for the door, but Grayson was hot on her heels. She needed to shake him. She needed to get away from absolutely everyone. She needed some time alone in order to think clearly.

The only person she really wanted to talk to was the one person missing from her life—her mother.

Not needing protection while she was within the palace walls, her security detail was out of sight. That left Grayson, who was right behind her. She kept moving with no particular destination in mind.

"Annabelle, you can't just walk away."

"Watch me."

"We need to talk."

"No, we don't." She kept walking, wishing he'd give up. "There's nothing to say."

"I disagree."

He refused to leave the subject alone. What did he want her to do? Say something to make it better? That wasn't possible.

Annabelle went out the back door. When she spotted her little red convertible, she headed straight for it. There wasn't anyone around, thankfully. She jumped inside and was relieved to find the keys waiting. The staff routinely left the keys in a strategic spot so that vehicles could be readily available and moved to the front of the palace for their owners. After all, the palace was heavily guarded. No one was going to break in and steal a car. Not a chance.

The next thing she knew, Grayson was in the seat next to her. *Just great.*

"You need to get out because I really am leaving."

"I'm not moving. You can't just act like nothing happened last night." He turned to her. "Annabelle, we have to talk."

"So you keep telling me." She put the car in gear. "Well, if you're not getting out, then I guess that means you're coming with me."

Grayson put on his seat belt, crossed his arms and then settled back in his seat. She'd never witnessed him with a more determined look.

"Don't say I didn't warn you." She accelerated toward the front gates.

It was then that she realized she didn't have her security detail following her. She also knew the guards would stop her and ask about her lack of security. She had no clue what to say. When she neared the gate, she found them opening it for a delivery truck. Though the guards waved for her to stop, she kept moving.

"Annabelle, what are you doing?"

"Whatever I want." She knew it was a childish answer, but she wasn't much in the mood for a serious talk.

It wasn't until they were on the main road that Grayson asked, "Would you at least tell me where we're going?"

"You'll find out soon enough."

"Annabelle?" Grayson stared into the passenger side mirror.

"I told you, you'll find out the destination soon."

"No, that isn't it." He tapped on the window. "There's no car behind us. Where's your security detail?"

He stared at her, waiting for this information to sink in. Her face paled as her gaze flicked to her rearview mirror. He knew she hadn't planned this little escapade. It'd been a spur-of-the-moment decision, which led him to believe she had been more upset this morning than she was willing to let on. He figured as much.

The thing was he wanted to talk to her. He wanted to tell her how much last night had meant to him, but she refused to give him a chance.

He'd have sworn by her responses and words that last night had been special for her too. So why had the walls gone up in the light of day? And what had she been doing up so early after such a late night?

That was his problem. He didn't understand women. He never had. Abbi used to tease him about it. But there was nothing funny about this situation—not after that threatening note.

"Annabelle, where's your security?"

"Obviously not here."

"I don't understand. Why would you leave without them?"

"Because…"

"Because what?" He wanted a real answer. What was going on with her? She'd been acting strange all morning.

"Because you wouldn't leave me alone. You kept wanting to talk about last night and I didn't. I didn't plan to leave the palace, at least not at that point and so I didn't tell anyone."

"You ran off?"

"No!" She frowned as her grip on the steering wheel visibly tightened. "I… I just didn't stop to tell anyone."

"Isn't that the same thing?"

She took her eyes off the road for a second to glare at him. "No. It isn't."

Grayson sighed. "Okay. I guess I did push the subject this morning. I'm sorry. I just thought we could talk things out." When she opened her mouth to protest, he continued before she could speak. "But no worries. Just turn around. We'll be back at the palace in no time."

Her lips pressed together. She didn't say anything and the car didn't slow down. Maybe she didn't hear him.

"Annabelle, turn around."

She eased up on the accelerator and the car started to slow down. He breathed easier. She'd turn around and soon they'd be back at the palace. No harm. No foul.

She put on the turn signal. So far so good. He glanced around. "What is this place?"

"It's a historic landmark. It's where our ancestor's fought to maintain our monarchy and traditions."

Any other time Grayson wouldn't have minded stopping and exploring the site, but not today. When Annabelle didn't immediately turn around, he thought she was just looking for a safe place to maneuver the car.

"You can turn here. I don't think there's anyone around to see if you drive off the road."

"I'm not turning around."

"What?"

"This is our destination."

"Annabelle, this isn't funny." A feeling of déjà vu came over him. "Turn around."

"No. We're here and there's something I need to see. It won't take long."

Arguing with her was proving fruitless so he pulled his cell phone from his pocket. He went to dial, but realized he didn't know the phone number of the palace. And that wasn't his only problem. There wasn't a signal out here in the middle of nowhere.

He held up his phone and waved it around. Not even one bar appeared on his phone. This wasn't good. He had a bad feeling about this whole expedition. A very bad feeling.

CHAPTER NINETEEN

THEY'D COME THIS FAR; she wasn't about to back away now.

"Come on." Annabelle got out of the car.

She wasn't so sure Grayson was going to accompany her. He was worried and she couldn't blame him, not after what he went through. But this wasn't her first time without a bodyguard and she highly doubted it would be her last. Sometimes she just needed some privacy and that was tough to do with someone always looking over your shoulder.

She glanced around. Hers was the only car in the parking lot. Everything would be all right. They wouldn't stay long. And contrary to her desires, she wasn't alone.

She started up the path leading to the historic landmark. The cipher had said *PLACARD. TWO. THREE*. Which, if this was the place, had to be just up ahead. She prayed she was right. She just wanted this to be over and to finally have the answers that would hopefully bring her family back together again.

"Annabelle, wait."

She paused and turned to find Grayson striding toward her. He wore a frown on his face that marred his handsomeness just a smidgen. And even if he wasn't happy about being here, she found comfort in his presence. Because maybe she wasn't feeling as brave as she'd like everyone to think. But she refused to be intimidated by that note. She was onto something; she just knew it.

"You're going to do this no matter what I say, aren't you?" His concerned gaze searched hers.

"I am."

He nodded. "Then lead the way."

"Thank you," she said, not expecting a response. But she was grateful that he wasn't going to fight her any longer.

They continued down the windy path that led them to a spot near the cliff that overlooked the sea. Here there was a small park area. There was a sign explaining the historic significance of the spot, but Annabelle wasn't up for a history lesson right now. She needed to see if this was the place with the next clue to her mother's murder and if not, they needed to move on.

"The message said there would be a placard. Do

you see one?" Annabelle gazed around the circular patio area. There were a few tables and benches scattered about. But she didn't see a placard.

Grayson was making his way around the circle. "Over here."

He was standing near a rock wall that butted up against a hillside at the back of the park. She rushed over to where he was standing. She looked around and found a bronze placard in the rock wall. It was dedicated to all of the heroes who had defended their homeland in 1714.

"Do you think that's it?" Annabelle's stomach shivered with nerves. Part of her wanted the truth but the other part of her worried about what she might learn. After all of this time, wondering and imagining what might have happened to her mother, she was surprised by her sudden hesitancy.

"Annabelle, what's wrong?" Grayson sent her a concerned look.

"Nothing." She was being silly. They had to find the answers. "Let's do this."

Grayson reached for her hand. "You do realize that this might not be the right place?"

She nodded. "But we won't know until we look."

Together they counted out the rocks, not quite sure where the starting point might be. The first try didn't pan out. The rock in the wall was firmly in there and there was no way they or anyone else was moving it without some serious tools. The second rock they tried had the same results.

"I'm starting to think I got the clues wrong," Annabelle said, feeling silly for taking Grayson on this pointless trip.

"Don't give up just yet. I think this rock is loose." Grayson gripped the stone and wiggled it. "Yes, it's definitely loose."

"This could be it." She moved forward, planning to help.

Before she could move into a position where she could reach the stone, Grayson jiggled it free. Her mouth gaped, but no words would come out. They'd found it. Would they at last have answers or find yet another coded message?

Grayson gestured toward the wall. "Well, don't just stand there, see if you can find anything."

His voice prompted her into action. She felt around inside the hole and grimaced when she realized there were bugs, slime and a whole host of other disgusting things in there. But then in the back of the cavity, her fingers ran across something different. Much different.

"I think there's a plastic bag in here."

"That's good. Can you pull it out?"

It was hung up in some soft dirt, but she easily

pulled it free. The bag was covered in muck, forcing Annabelle to swipe it off with her hand if she had any hope of seeing what was inside.

"Is there anything else in there?" Grayson asked.

"Just this. It looks like some sort of thumb drive. An older one."

Grayson returned the rock to its spot and then moved next to her. She handed over the bag. All the while, she wondered what could be so important about a computer file that it cost her mother her life.

"What do you think is on it?" Annabelle asked.

"I don't know, but I'm guessing it's very important."

"It is," a male voice said from behind them. "Now turn around slowly."

Dread inched down Annabelle's spine like icy fingers. When she turned, she gasped. The man standing there holding a gun on them was someone she knew—someone the king knew and trusted. It was one of the palace staff, Mr. Drago.

He was an older man with thinning white hair and the gun he held on them looked to be even older than him. The hand holding the large revolver shook, but she didn't know if it was from nerves or age. Either way, she wasn't feeling so good about his finger resting on the trigger.

"Drop the bag to the ground and kick it over here," he demanded.

Grayson did as he said without any argument.

"And now your keys."

Annabelle had those. She pulled them from her pocket and dropped them to the ground. She gave them a swift kick sending them skidding over the concrete patio.

"Why?" Annabelle hadn't meant to speak—to do anything to provoke him, but the word popped out of her mouth before she could stop it. With the damage already done, she asked, "Why did you kill my mother?"

After the man picked up the plastic bag and the keys, he stuffed them in his pocket. "You don't understand." His eyes filled with emotion. "No one was supposed to get hurt."

The tremors in his hand grew more intense. The gun moved up and down, left and right. And yet his finger remained on the trigger.

"Your mother, she just wouldn't quit interfering. Just like you. I warned you to leave the past alone, but you just couldn't."

"I...I just need to know the truth—to understand." Annabelle couldn't believe she was staring at the man who had killed her mother. Nothing about the man screamed murderer to her and yet, he'd almost come right out and admitted it. "Why did she have to die?"

The man expelled a weary sigh as though he were shouldering the weight of the world. "Since I'm leaving this island—my home—and never coming back, I suppose I can tell you. My wife… she was sick. She needed to be flown to the United States for treatment, but I didn't have that kind of money. And then I got an offer. For some information about the country's defenses, I could get the money necessary to save my wife's life. I'd have done anything for her. She…she was my world."

Annabelle helplessly stared at the man who'd murdered her mother. His hand with the gun continued to shake. And his finger remained on the trigger. Anger and disbelief churned in her gut. And worst yet, she'd dragged Grayson into this mess, risking both of their lives. She deeply regretted her rash decision to rush out here without security.

There had to be a way out of this. Maybe if she kept the man talking a bit longer, a plan would come to mind. "So what went wrong?"

"Your mother caught on to the plan somehow. She said she was going to tell the king, and I just couldn't let her ruin everything."

And then a memory fell into place. "It was you

that I saw arguing with her in the South Shore piazza the evening before she died, wasn't it?"

He nodded. "I was trying to find out how much she knew. I needed to know if she suspected me. She wouldn't tell me anything, but then the next day we met again. She said she'd intercepted a note to me—"

"Your name is Cosmo?" For as long as Annabelle had been coming to the palace, she'd only ever heard the man addressed by his surname—Drago.

"Yes, it is." His arm slowly lowered as though he was tired of holding up the gun. In the next breath, he lifted it again. "Your mother said that she was taking it to the king. That's when I pulled out this gun. She reached for it. We struggled and…and it went off. There was nothing I could do for the princess. The shot hit her in the chest. She…she died before she hit the ground."

Annabelle's heart jumped into her throat as she envisioned her mother's final moments. Her mother had been protecting the king and this land that she loved. She was a hero and no one knew until now.

Annabelle swallowed hard. "What…what happened next?"

"My wife…she died before I could get the data to sell."

"And what's on this thumb drive?"

"Instructions on where to deliver the data. And how I'd get my payments."

"So you never met the person behind the espionage?"

"No. There were cryptic messages and a couple of phone calls."

"And they just left you alone after your wife died? Even though they didn't get their information?"

"I was a man with nothing to lose and nothing to gain by then. I told the man on the phone that I'd go to the king and take my punishment before I'd give in to his blackmail."

"Funny how you grew a conscience after my mother died." Annabelle's hands clenched at her sides as she tried to keep her emotions under control. "How could you do that? Do you know how much we loved and needed her?"

The older man's eyes grew shiny with unshed tears and his face creased with worry lines. "I told you I didn't mean for it to happen. It…it was an accident."

"And then what? You made it look like a mugging gone wrong?"

Drago's eyes narrowed. "What choice did I have?

I couldn't go to jail. Not with my wife so ill. And it was an accident."

The man didn't even hesitate as he spoke. Annabelle's mouth gaped. The man seemed to think of himself as innocent. No wonder he'd gotten away with it for so many years. Without a guilty conscience to trip him up, it'd been easy.

"What did you do with my mother's jewelry?" Perhaps it was stashed in the palace and could be used as evidence.

"I buried it."

"Where?"

"I…I don't know. It was a long time ago."

"And you just stayed on at the palace, serving the king and acting like nothing ever happened?"

"What else could I do?" A tear splashed onto his weathered cheek. "The king needed me. I couldn't let him down."

But you could kill his sister without batting an eye? Annabelle wanted to tell Mr. Drago about the devastation he'd caused, but she had Grayson's safety to think about. She couldn't agitate this man any further. And there was nothing he could say that would bring her mother back to them.

And that was when she noticed movement behind Mr. Drago.

"What are you planning to do with us?" Grayson asked.

She figured that he must have seen her security team and the police moving into position behind the man. And Grayson was doing his best to distract Drago until they were ready to make their move.

"Do with you?" The man's face broke into a smile. "You think I'm going to kill you too?"

What did one say to that in this very sensitive situation? Annabelle glanced at Grayson, willing him not to upset the man, who was obviously not quite all there.

Grayson shrugged. "I don't know."

"I'm just going to leave you stranded out here. No one ever visits this place. I'm surprised you found it."

"How did you discover we were coming here?"

"It wasn't hard to eavesdrop and do a bit of snooping—"

His words were cut off as the police signaled for Annabelle and Grayson to drop to the ground. Grayson leapt into action shielding Annabelle's body with his own. Seconds felt like minutes as she was trapped between the concrete and Grayson's muscled chest.

"All clear," an officer called out.

Grayson helped her to her feet. "Are you all right?"

Annabelle nodded. With unshed tears blurring her vision, she said, "I'm so, so sorry. I never meant for any of this to happen."

He didn't say anything. In fact, without another word, he turned his back to her. She blinked repeatedly as she watched him walk away. She had a sickening feeling that, although no shots had been fired, there had been a casualty today.

Their relationship.

CHAPTER TWENTY

THE RIDE BACK to the palace was tense and silent.

However, the scene awaiting Annabelle was anything but.

They didn't even make it past the great foyer before her father, followed by the king, confronted her. One glance at Grayson told her that she was in this alone. He wouldn't look at her, much less speak to her. They were acting like she'd planned for all of this to happen. All she'd wanted were some long-overdue answers. Was that so bad?

Speaking of answers, she didn't even get a chance to tell them that she finally had them—she knew what had happened—before her father launched into a heated speech.

"How could you do this?" Her father's face was flushed and his arms gestured as he spoke. "I thought I could trust you. And here you go, sneaking around, risking your safety."

"You don't understand—"

"Oh, I understand." Her father frowned at her

before stepping in front of Grayson, who at least had the common sense to stay quiet during this confrontation. "And you, I expected more of you. And yet, you let my daughter go off recklessly without her security—"

"That was not my doing." Grayson's voice rumbled with agitation. "At least it wasn't intentionally. We both got wrapped up in a heated conversation. By the time I realized that Annabelle had forgotten proper protocol, we were almost at the landmark."

Her father's voice echoed throughout the foyer. "How could you not realize you were leaving without any security?"

Grayson and her father glared at each other. Jaws were tight. Hands were clenched.

The king cleared his throat. "We were just really worried about you when your bodyguard reported that you'd slipped off without notifying anyone."

Her father's mouth opened, but before he could utter another angry word, Annabelle said, "And how exactly did you find us if my security wasn't following me?"

Her father paused. He averted his gaze. She knew this reaction. She'd seen it in the past when he'd done something that he knew his family would not approve of.

"Poppa, what is it? What did you do?"

His gaze met hers. "It was for your own good. I knew you were out of control and that things might end badly. I had to protect you."

"Poppa, out with it."

He sighed. "After I learned that you stole your mother's journal—"

"Borrowed."

"Fine. Borrowed. I knew there was a possibility that you'd get caught up in the past and you wouldn't be able to stop yourself—you'd have to follow the clues."

"Of course. How could you expect me not to?"

"Well, I wasn't about to let you go off and get yourself hurt so I installed a tracking device in your purse and your car, as well as a tracking app on your phone. I wasn't taking any chances."

Annabelle checked her phone. "You really did. How could you?"

"What? You're attacking me. My forethought is what saved your life."

Annabelle reached for Grayson's hand, craving his strength and the knowledge that they were in this together. Her fingers brushed over the back of his hand. She was just about to curl her fingers around his when he moved his hand behind his back out of her reach.

When she glanced his way, Grayson was staring straight ahead. She couldn't look into his eyes. She had no way of discovering why he had gone from being so helpful at the landmark to completely shutting down now that they were back at the palace. And the little voice in the back of her mind was warning her this was something different from his confrontation with her father. This thing, whatever it was, had to do with her and her alone.

She turned back to her expectant parent. "Mr. Drago wasn't going to hurt us."

When the king spoke, his voice was hollow as though he were in shock. "Drago, he admitted everything to you?"

Annabelle nodded. "I had to push him a bit, but in the end, it all came out."

"Oh, my." The king's color was sickly white. He stumbled a bit. Grayson and her father rushed to his side and helped him into a chair.

"I'll get help," Annabelle said, afraid this revelation was too much for her uncle.

"No. I'm fine," the king said in an unsteady voice. "I don't believe this. First my wife is murdered and now, my sister—all in the name of the crown." His head sunk into his hands.

Annabelle's heart went out to the man, who had weathered so much during his reign. She'd been so young when her aunt, the queen, was assassinated. The assailant had been aiming for the king but had missed. The whole ordeal had taken a toll on the family, but justice had been carried out. Who'd have imagined a few years later Annabelle's own mother would be killed.

Sometimes she thought being royal was a blessing and other times, she knew that it was a curse. Because the king was right, if not for the crown, both of the women who had meant so much to him—to all of them—would still be here.

"I think that it was an accident," Annabelle said, hoping to lessen the blow for everyone.

"Annabelle, how can you talk like this?" Her father's voice shook with emotion. "He stole your mother from us. Surely you must hate him?"

She shook her head. "No, not hate."

"I don't understand," her father said. "I'm trying, but I just don't get it."

She recalled the time she'd spent with her mother. They hadn't enjoyed many years together but in the time that they'd had, her mother taught her some valuable life lessons. "I don't think Momma would want any of us to hate Mr. Drago. She used to say that hate, and even the word itself, was a more powerful weapon than anything man could ever create. Hate could destroy a man as sure as it could destroy a nation."

Her father's mouth gaped as he tried to absorb his daughter's words. And then he composed himself. "For a moment there, you sounded just like her. I never knew she told you that. I'd almost forgotten that she'd said it. And so you've forgiven this Drago man?"

Annabelle shook her head. "Right now, I'm struggling with the not hating part. Forgiveness, well, it's a long ways off. He stole a very precious person from me—from all of us. And then he nearly destroyed our family by covering it up. He did a lot of damage, but I'm trying to take comfort in knowing he now has to account for his crimes."

"I don't know." Her father rubbed the back of his neck. "I don't think I can be as calm and rational about this as you."

She didn't want to lose her father again to hatred and resentment. Maybe if she explained a little more, it would help. "He said he never meant to hurt her, just scare her. And the gun accidentally fired."

Her father looked at her with disbelief reflected in his eyes. "And you believed him?"

She nodded. "He was leaving the country and

never coming back. I'm not even sure that old gun still worked. What do you think, Grayson?"

Instead of answering her, he turned and walked away.

Where was he going? And why wasn't he speaking to her?

She chased after him, following him up the stairs. She couldn't let him get away. Not now. Not after everything that they'd shared. This was the beginning. Not the end.

Grayson couldn't stand there for one more minute.

It didn't matter what anyone said to Annabelle; she thought that she had done the right thing. He'd only ever been that scared one other time in his life. He'd sworn he would never live through something like it again. And yet just minutes ago he'd been staring down the end of a gun and praying that nothing would happen to Annabelle. And she'd refused to be quiet. She'd kept pushing the man, agitating him.

Grayson's heart pounded just recalling the horrific scene. Why did he think that staying here was a good idea? Why did he think Annabelle would be different?

He strode down the hallway toward his suite of rooms. He needed to get away—to be alone. A headache was pounding in his temples. His neck and shoulders ached. His muscles had been tense since he realized they'd left the palace without her security.

He'd just stepped in his room when he heard Annabelle calling out his name. Couldn't she get the message? He just wanted to be alone.

"Grayson—"

"Not now. Go away." He looked around for his bag. He needed to start packing. He just couldn't stay here any longer.

She didn't say anything for a moment and he was hoping that she'd take the hint and leave. He needed to calm down so he didn't end up saying anything that he would later regret.

"I can't go. I don't understand what's going on." She stepped further into the room.

"You don't understand?" Was she serious?

She sent him a wide-eyed stare. "Why are you so upset?"

"Because of you." At last, he recalled his bag was in the closet. He retrieved it and threw it on the bed. "You're reckless. You think you're invincible. And you don't listen to anyone."

"If this is about earlier, I'm sorry. I was just doing what I thought was best—"

"Best for you. Not best for anyone who cares

about you. If that man had shot you…" No, he wasn't going there. He couldn't think about going through that agonizing pain again.

He went to the chest of drawers and retrieved a handful of clothes. The sooner he packed, the sooner he'd be on his way to the airport.

"Grayson, what are you doing?"

"I'm packing. I'm leaving here. I should have left a long time ago."

"But…but what about us?"

He didn't stop moving—he couldn't. He stuffed his clothes haphazardly in the bag. As soon as he was out of here—away from Mirraccino—he'd be able to breathe. The worry, it would cease.

"Grayson?"

He kept packing. In the long run, she'd be better off without him. "There is no us. I can't—I won't—continue this relationship. You take too many needless chances. I can't be a part of your life."

"Seriously?" Anger threaded through her voice. "I did what I had to do. And you know it."

"I know you took a chance with your life—with both of our lives. And it wasn't necessary. The police could have handled it."

Out of the corner of his eye, he spied her pressing her hands to her hips. He didn't dare look at her face. He couldn't stand to see the pain that would be reflected in her eyes—pain he'd put there.

"Don't you understand? The police never would have gotten to the truth. Without it my family would never heal."

Part of him knew she believed the words she uttered. Her entire family was separated with no true hope of coming back together. This discovery would give them a chance to start over.

But he also knew that taking risks and breaking rules was what had cost Abbi her life. He couldn't stick around and wait for Annabelle to take another risk. He couldn't stand the thought of losing her just like he'd lost Abbi.

"Grayson, are you even listening to me?" Annabelle moved to the other side of the bed, trying to gain his attention. "Are you leaving because you never really cared about me?"

It was in that moment he realized he was leaving for the exact opposite reason.

He loved Annabelle.

Normally that revelation would bring someone joy and delight, but it made his blood run cold. He'd cared deeply about Abbi, but he'd never loved her like this.

But with Annabelle, he was head over heels in love. The acknowledgment scared him silly. It didn't matter what she promised, she now had the power to destroy him—to rip his heart to shreds.

"I…I can't do this, Annabelle. I'm sorry." He zipped his bag closed, grabbed his computer case from where he kept it on the desk and headed for the door.

He paused in the doorway. Unable to face her, he kept his back to her. "I know you won't believe this, but I did care. I do care. You're just too reckless. I thought we had a chance but I was wrong. I'm glad you found the truth, but now I have to go."

There was a sniffle behind him, but he couldn't help her now. The best thing he could do for both of them was to start walking and keep going. Because the one thing he'd learned in life was that people let you down, sometimes without even meaning to.

This was for the best.

But it sure didn't feel like it. Not at all.

With each step the ache in his heart increased.

CHAPTER TWENTY-ONE

ALONE.

Not a soul around.

Annabelle made her way along the deserted beach with the bright moonlight guiding her. She had no destination in mind. There was no place she needed to be. And no one who was expecting her.

She should be kicking up her heels and savoring this moment. Or at the very least feeling as though she'd gained something huge—her freedom. There were no longer people looking over her shoulder. There were no reports filed with her father, detailing any of her activities. And that's because the security detail had been officially dismissed not long after Drago was arrested.

Annabelle stopped walking and turned to the water. It wasn't until that moment she realized her freedom was not what she'd been truly craving all of this time. Because if it was then she wouldn't feel so utterly alone and adrift.

Grayson was gone.

For a moment after he'd packed his bags and walked out the door, she'd thought he might change his mind. She'd prayed that he would come back to her. She'd assured herself that he was just having some sort of reaction to the scene at the landmark. Maybe it was shock or fear and it would pass. It didn't.

But how could he just walk away? He did care about her. Didn't he?

There had been lunches and dinners. The chariot race. The gown he'd given her. Their collaboration over the coded messages. And there were so many small moments...a look here or a touch there. Didn't those all add up to mean something special?

Or had she just been fooling herself?

Maybe if she'd been more open, more honest about her feelings for him instead of keeping it all locked safely inside. Maybe if she'd have taken a chance, he'd still be here.

A breeze off the water rushed over her skin and combed through her hair. She folded her arms over her chest and rubbed her arms with her palms. At last, she realized that freedom wasn't something anyone could give her. Real freedom came from living her life to its fullest and opening her heart to others—something she'd never done with any man—including Grayson.

She missed him so much that her heart ached. There was a gaping hole in it and she didn't know how to stop the pain. By now, he'd be on his way to Italy or California.

How was it that this man had crashed into her life on a city sidewalk and so quickly, so easily snuck past all of her defenses and burrowed so deeply into her heart? And how did she learn to live without his warm smiles, his deep laughs and his gentle touch?

She groaned with frustration. This was a time when a girl really needed her mother. Tears blurred Annabelle's vision and she blinked them away. What would her mother say to her?

Would her mother ask her how she'd fallen so hard? Would she want to know how Annabelle had mucked things up so quickly? And what would she say to her mother? Would she blame it on the severe restrictions her father had unfairly placed upon her? Or would she take responsibility herself for what had happened?

How had she let all of this happen? How had she let herself fall in love only to lose him so quickly?

And then to her horror, she realized her father hadn't put her in a gilded cage, she'd done that all by herself—she'd done it by keeping everyone in her life at arm's length. If she truly wanted to be free, she had to be willing to open her heart…the whole way.

In that moment, alone on the moonlit beach, she knew what she had to do next. It was time she took that long-thought-about trip to the United States.

But she wouldn't be running away—she'd be running toward something—or rather toward someone.

CHAPTER TWENTY-TWO

AT LAST HE WAS on his way.

Grayson had stood for a very long time outside the gates of the palace waiting for the taxi to pick him up, at least an hour, if not longer. When he'd first called for a ride and given them the address, they'd thought he was joking. They had no idea that joking around was the very last thing on his mind.

It was almost as if fate was giving him time to change his mind—time to calm down. Well, he had calmed down. The panic over how close Annabelle had come to being hurt had passed.

But what hadn't passed was his determination to leave here—leave Annabelle. They didn't belong together. They came from very different worlds and he had no idea how to fit into hers. And she was too reckless for him to even consider sharing something serious with her.

He'd thought that by walking away from Annabelle he would start to feel better. After all, he'd cut things off. He'd protected himself and her.

Now, in a taxi, speeding toward Mirraccino International Airport, Grayson leaned his head back against the seat. He assured himself that he was doing the right thing. So why did he feel so awful?

He sighed. He'd already decided to cancel the rest of his Mediterranean trip. The expansion project would go on, but he'd put someone else in charge. He needed some distance from the sunny shores, blue waters and everything else that reminded him of Annabelle.

She was reckless with her safety. He couldn't be with someone like that. He needed someone in his life who was...what? Cautious? Sedate? Anything that wasn't Annabelle.

And why did he need that?

He didn't want to examine the answer too closely. He worried about what he might find when he pulled back the layers. Because it wasn't Annabelle who had the problems.

It was him.

As the airport came into sight, Grayson could no longer run from the truth. He had to accept that he was at fault here—not Annabelle. The moment of truth had arrived. He could either take the easy way out or he could do what was right.

The taxi pulled up to the curb outside the terminal. "Sir, we're here."

Grayson didn't respond. Nor did he move.

By flying off into the night, he was doing what he'd accused Annabelle of doing—being reckless.

Not that he was being reckless with his safety, rather he was being reckless with his heart. True love didn't come around all that often and for him to turn his back on it was wrong. Because whether it was convenient, sensible, or for that matter logical, he was in love with the duke's daughter.

"Please take me back to the palace."

Would it be too late?

Would she at least hear him out?

He had to hope so.

CHAPTER TWENTY-THREE

ANNABELLE'S MIND WAS made up.

Now all there was to do was make her flight reservations and pack her bags.

There was no time to waste. Every moment that she knew Grayson was upset with her was torture. She didn't even know if he'd open the door to her, but she had to try. She couldn't live with the what-ifs.

Annabelle trudged through the sand toward the steps that climbed up the cliff behind the palace. As for her father and uncle, she'd have to tell them something, but she didn't know exactly what to say or when to say it—

A movement caught her attention. She glanced up at the top of the steps. She could see the shadowed outline of a person. Who would be coming out here this evening? With her cousins and their families still off on their trips, it didn't leave many people who frequented the beach.

As she studied the figure now moving down the

steps at a rapid pace, she made out that it was a man. The breath caught in her throat. Was it possible that it was Grayson? Had he changed his mind? Had he come back for her?

Her heart swelled with hope. A part of her knew that if it was indeed him, then he could have come back for a number of reasons including cancelling his contract for the Fo Shizzle Café.

Please say it isn't so.

Not about to wait, she started up the steps. The closer she got to him, the more certain she was that it was Grayson. This was her chance to fix things. Now she had to pray that she'd find the right words to convince him that they deserved another chance.

She moved up the steps as fast as her legs would allow. Breathless and nervous, she came face-to-face with Grayson on the middle landing. Her gaze met his, but she wasn't able to read his thoughts.

"I'm sorry." They both said in unison.

Had she heard him correctly? She wanted to rush into his arms, but she restrained herself. She had to be sure he wanted the same things as her.

"I never meant to scare you," she said. "When I went to the landmark, I never imagined that anyone would find us there. I'm sorry."

He continued to stare into her eyes. "And I overreacted. I was afraid that something would happen

to you. And I just couldn't handle that because…
because I love you."

Her heart swelled with joy. "You do?"

He nodded. "I do. I love you too much for you to
take unnecessary chances with your safety."

"I promise to be more cautious going forward
because I always want to be able to go home to
the man I love."

Grayson opened his arms up to her and she
rushed into them.

"I love you," she murmured into his ear.

"I love you too."

At last, she had the love she'd always dreamed of.

Life didn't get any better than this.

EPILOGUE

Two months later...

"GRAYSON, WHAT ARE WE doing here?"

Annabelle stood next to the water fountain in the piazza of the South Shore. She was all dressed up as she'd been in business meetings off and on all morning. Grayson knew this because he'd had a horrible time trying to reach her. At one point, he'd feared that his surprise would be ruined. But at last, he'd heard her voice on the other end of the phone and begged her to meet him here.

He smiled at her. "Don't you know what today is?"

"Of course I do. It's Wednesday."

"True. But it's something else. Something very special."

"Aren't you supposed to break ground for your new offices?"

"Done."

She clasped her hands together and smiled. "Great. Is that what you wanted to show me?"

He shook his head. He had fun surprising her and he'd made a point of it over the past two months, from flowers to chocolate to the sweetest kitten. But today, this would be the biggest surprise of all.

She sent him a puzzled look. "Grayson, what are you up to?"

"Do I need to be up to something?"

She studied him for a moment. "You're most definitely up to something." She smiled. "Are you going to tell me? Or do I need to keep guessing?"

This was the moment. He dropped down on one knee. "Lady Annabelle, you captured my heart the first time we stood next to this fountain. You've led me on an amazing journey. You've taught me how to love. And you've made me the happiest man in the world."

Annabelle gasped and pressed a shaky hand to her gaping mouth. Her eyes glistened with unshed tears of joy. All around them a crowd of curious onlookers was gathering, but it didn't faze him. All that mattered now was Annabelle.

He pulled a little black box from his pocket. He opened it and held it up to her. "Annabelle, I love you. Will you be my best friend, my partner, my lover, forever?"

The tears streamed onto her cheeks as she nodded and smiled.

He placed the ring on her finger before he swept her into his arms and kissed her. He would never tire of holding her close.

When she pulled back, she gazed up at him. "You really want to do this? Get married?"

He nodded. "Definitely. I'm thinking we'll have a grand wedding. We could have it right here, if you like."

"Here in the piazza?" She didn't look so sure. "How about we think it over? After all, I don't want to rush this. I plan to be engaged only once and I want a chance to savor it."

"Then how would you feel about the grandest engagement party?"

Her face lit up. "I love it! But the size of the party doesn't matter as long as all of the men in my life are there."

"Then it's a plan. I love you."

"I love you too."

* * * * *